Lines of Fire

By

Janet Lane Walters

ISBN: 9781482736847

Books We Love Ltd.
Chestermere, Alberta
Canada

Copyright 2012 by Janet Lane Walters
Cover Art 2012 by Michelle Lee

All rights reserved. Without limiting the rights under copyright reserved above, no part of this publication may be reproduced, stored in or introduced into a retrieval system, or transmitted in any form, or by any means (electronic, mechanical, photocopying, recording, or otherwise) without the prior written permission of both the copyright owner and the above publisher of this book.

Lines of Fire
Page 2

DEDICATION

Lines of Fire
Page 4

The Guild House Series

Defenders Hall
Lines of Fire

Prologue

Whispers of the grief to come slithered through Alric's thoughts. He knelt beside his father's bed and brushed the older man's hand. The lines of fire on his father's skin, once bright scarlet, had faded to pale pink. Though the end approached, Alric wasn't ready to see his father pass from life into the abyss of death.

"Papa," he whispered. "The men of the Guild House and their bondmates arrive in just five days to test me for admission into the Defenders Hall." His words were a plea for his father to remain with him for that time.

The older man's eyes opened. The pain Alric saw brought wetness to his eyes. When his father died, there would be no relative to witness the acceptance as a Defender trainee. From the moment his father had given Alric a wooden sword and shown him the ways one could be used, he had desired to leave the village and pursue more training.

With fierce determination, Alric sought to infuse some of his vitality into his father. As always, the attempt failed. Why could the lines of fire be used to halt the flow of blood and to not achieve a return to vitality? Alric groaned. If he had been on the wood-cutting trip into the forest, he could have helped his father and the other man. A boar had gored and broken their bodies. The other lumberman had died. Alric's father had lingered and suffered.

"Son."

The harsh whisper startled Alric. His father hadn't spoken once in the ten days since his shattered body had been carried to the village.

"Papa."

"Listen. Be Defender."

"I promise."

"Swordmaster. Enemy. Lines of fire. Not all can see." Alric frowned. What did his father mean? Was the Swordmaster the reason his father's bond had been broken and he had been banished to this distant village? Why should the lines remain a secret? Before he had a chance to ask his father spoke again.

"Find sibs."

Alric's head jerked up. "Sibs. I have none."

"One boy. One girl. Too young to steal away. Just you."

This new information rocked Alric's thoughts. "I will find them."

"Bracelet. Take. Use. True mate."

New ideas and new demands swamped Alric. Questions rattled like nuts falling from the trees in autumn.

"Save. Defenders. Restore old ways. Promise."

"I will." Alric wasn't sure what he had promised but his father's words flowed through his thoughts the way the lines of fire flowed over his skin. He pressed his forehead against his father's hand and slammed shut the gates of grief.

The rattled breathing slowed and began again. Each stop and start brought a welling of tears closer to the surface. The sound stopped. Alric waited. He raised his head. The lines of fire on his father's skin vanished.

Gut churning sobs began and wracked Alric's body. When the storm of tears stopped Alric rose. With leaden steps he walked to the cabin door to summon the village women to care for his father's corpse.

* * *

On the day of testing, Alric waited with the other youths on the village commons. He had his father's knife, sword and bonding bracelet. As he stared down the road, he recited the names of the four Guilds and their colors.

"Healers, blue. Justicars, black. Artisans, motley in red, purple and yellow. Defenders green."

Around him whispers rose until they became a steady buzz like swarming bees. "Here they come."

He studied the riders and their mounts. Four men and four women approached the village. The twin horns of the steeds had been polished until they gleamed. The coats of the bihorns varied in color from cream to sable.

By the end of the day, Alric bristled with pride. He had fulfilled one of the promises made to his father. He was the only one of the boys chosen to train as a Defender. Two girls had been tapped to become Defenders. He wondered why they had been chosen.

Neither had any weapon skills.

Before leaving the village with the youths selected for the four guilds, he slipped away from the celebration to visit his father's grave. Silent tears fell. He dashed them away. "In five years I'll wear Defender's green. I will keep the promises I made."

Chapter 1

The challenge match had lasted longer than Alric thought possible. His opponent, one of the desert riders, had been chosen by his clan for the duel. Only one man could win. If Alric bested the other fighter, the local farmers would be spared raids on their crops and herds by the nomad band comprised of rebels against the laws of Investia. If he lost the raids would continue until another patrol arrived. Alric concentrated on the lines of fire flowing over the other man's skin.

The younger man was agile and talented with the sword and knife. His hair, bleached by the sun, shone red-gold in the morning light. The lines flowed in changing scarlet patterns over his arms and bare chest.

Alric's opponent's quick responses to each move made him believe the young man read the lines, too. Someone had to make a mistake before they collapsed.

Sweat coated Alric's skin. An occasional droplet stung his eyes and blurred his vision. The desert rider showed the same physical reactions. Exhaustion threatened Alric's control. Then he found an opening. The lines of fire on the younger man's sword hand faltered.

Alric lunged and caught the other sword sending the blade sailing through the air. He followed with a sweep of his leg. The desert rider sprawled on the ground. Alric pressed his knife against the man's pulsing neck vein.

"Yield," he demanded.

"Yielded." The young man grinned. "Good fight. I'm Jens."

"Alric."

Jens turned to the gathered clansmen and the crowd of cheering farmers. "Trade is good unless you try to cheat. We have wool, silver, gold, some gemstones, herbs and spices. We need grain, produce, honey and beer."

"Do you have salt among the spices?" a man asked.

"We do."

Moments later someone tapped a keg of beer. Alric opted for a mug of water. Once the formalities ended he searched the crowd for his current bondmate. Before he found her, Jens beckoned. They drew apart from the celebrating clan and villagers.

"I gather you see the lines of fire," Jens said.

Alric glanced around to make sure no one stood close enough to hear. "It is said only those who are heart bound can see them. Among the Defenders I do not speak of my ability to anyone other than those I trust."

"Why? I have no bondmate and my friends know of my ability. That's why I'm chosen for these duels. You're my first loss."

Alric moved further from the celebration. "Seeing the lines is one of the reasons our forefathers used the mists to come to this land. Sorcerers sought to use their talents for evil."

"An old wives' tale I've often heard from the elderly riders."

"Perhaps. I'm a Defender as I promised my father I would become. I believe what he told me when I was growing up."

Jens frowned. "How fortunate to have known your father. As a small child I lived in the Defenders Hall. My mother died so I was fostered to a shepherd's family when I was three. Soon as I could I ran. A penned life isn't for me."

Alric swallowed. "Did you have a sister?"

Jens shrugged. "My memories of the Defenders Hall are poor. What I remember is a tall man dragging me away and riding with him for days."

Alric wished the younger man had more memories but he feared he would never know if this young man was his lost brother. "You might consider coming with our patrol. Though you're older than most of the trainees, your skill would let you advance rapidly."

Jens laughed. "You could leave the Defenders behind and join this clan of riders. We would welcome a man with your skills. You and I could be invincible as a team at the games."

Alric studied the ground. There were times when he dreamed of leaving the Defenders. Some of the twelve years hadn't been pleasant, especially when the leader placed obstacles in his way. He'd leaped over those stumbling blocks and succeeded. The promise he'd made to his father ruled his life.

Alric turned away and saw his bondmate waving. "I must go. Good riding and successful dueling."

"Same."

When Alric strode away from the younger man he scowled. The connection to Jens had been deeper than usual. Though the younger man had no memories of the past, he could be one of the missing sibs. In an instant Alric decided when he returned to the Hall he would search the Archives to see if the records held any information about his family.

His bondmate led him away from the crowd. "Where is the rest of the patrol?" he asked.

"I told them to head out and you would catch up."

She wore no bracelet. A groan rumbled from his gut. Bracelets meant the bonding between mates stood. Since she had removed hers, that meant he'd been twice rejected. Once more and he would be banished from the Defenders. He opened the clasp on the brass one he wore.

"Seeks you won't be returning with me."

She stared at the ground. "I never wanted to be a Defender. I wanted to exchange bracelets with my childhood sweetheart. He's here and wears no bracelet."

With his thumbs, Alric tilted her head to see her expression. Though her decision was right for her, sadness shrouded his thoughts. "I wish you happiness." He dropped the bracelet she had clasped on his wrist during the bonding ceremony into her hand. "Here's your price."

She shook her head. "I don't want you to pay the fine. I never tried to see if our bond could last."

"Neither did I."

"You could have forced me to unite with you."

Alric grimaced. "I wasn't raised to grab what I wasn't offered."

"What will you do?" she asked.

"The patrol has finished the rounds of the southern sector of Investia. The Day of Ingathering for the returning patrols is just weeks away. I'll ride to the Defenders Hall and choose another mate."

"I wish you luck."

Alric walked away. He touched the bracelet hidden beneath his shirt. His father had given him the unique piece just before his death. Perhaps this time he would find his heart bound mate.

* * *

Not wanting to admit his second failure to find a bondmate, Alric held his bihorn, Storm Cloud to a walk and avoided farms and villages. At night he camped in forest glades. Though the members of his patrol wouldn't blame him for the failure he felt troubled. Somewhere in the Hall his heart bound waited for discovery. Would he have the time to find her or would the Swordmaster force him to make another unsuitable choice?

Two weeks after leaving the site of the duel with the desert rider, Alric neared the Guild House. He pushed his bihorn to a steady pace. By late afternoon he would reach his destination. Three days after that, Ingathering Day would occur. The other four patrols had already left on their rounds. When he arrived he had to report to the Swordmaster and face the leader's gloating remarks over the failure of another bonding.

Tension centered between his shoulder blades. He pressed a hand against the bonding bracelet dangling from a chain about his neck. The links of the unusual piece were made from gold, silver, copper and electrum.

The sun reached midday. Storm Cloud slowed. Alric stroked his mount's neck. "Not much further. Then grooming, food and a treat."

The steed's pace returned to a steady canter. Alric steadied his thoughts. He would reach the Hall in time to search the records for news of the sibs his father had mentioned years ago. He had avoided searching before but since meeting Jens, a need to know had arisen.

When he saw the massive stone wall surrounding the four halls belonging to the four guilds of Investia, foreboding entered his thoughts. Though his father had named the Swordmaster as an enemy, Alric didn't understand the older man's animosity. During the training days there had never been a word of praise. Even now Alric's reports were searched for flaws.

He rode through the open gate leading to the Defenders Hall. He dismounted and led his bihorn across the courtyard to the stables. There he brushed Storm Cloud's dark brown coat until it gleamed, polished the horns and checked the animal's hooves. He filled the manger with hay and oats, adding a handful of the tart purple apelons. These fruits were the steed's favorite treat.

After cleaning and oiling the saddle and tack, he hung them on a hook and lifted the pack and journal. Unable to delay any longer he strode to the central entrance. He paused outside the Swordmaster's door and knocked. He braced for the lecture he didn't deserve. Neither of his bondmates chosen by the leader had suited. They had returned to their villages. Though the leader should guard his men, the Swordmaster's attempts to control Alric's life were wrong.

"Enter."

Alric closed the door and stood in front of the highly polished mahogany desk. The dark wood was covered with record books. The Swordmaster glared. A liberal sprinkling of white, colored his sandy hair.

"Defender Alric, reporting." He placed his journal on the desk.

The Swordmaster bent his head and read the short entries. "Your accounts agree with the others of your patrol. No fatalities and only one death among your four years on rounds of the sectors. You have quite a record." He stroked his chin. "Why do young men not chosen for training attack from behind?"

Alric shrugged. "If I could read minds such tragedies could be avoided."

"Where is your bondmate?"

Alric straightened. "She remained at the outpost village in the southern sector. She had no desire to be a Defender and her skills were mediocre." He placed his hands on the desk. "This time the choice is mine."

The older man's jaw thrust forward. "There is no time for you to visit the Women's Quarters and court any of the unbonded. There are important short assignments you can best fulfill. I have chosen the perfect mate for you. She has long admired your skills and she will bond permanently. When she names you,

you will accept."

Alric drew a deep breath. "According to the rules governing this guild, a man or a woman has the right to choose his third mate. Section 4, Rule 1."

The older man smiled. "Rules can be overturned by the Swordmaster."

A frown tightened Alric's forehead. He had memorized the Defender's rules. "Why have I never seen that written?"

"Unwritten and known only to the Swordmaster. Passed from my predecessor to me. Followed for several generations. Broken just once in my memory and the Defender who broke the rule ended in disgrace. The woman he chose walked into the abyss of death."

Though Alric fought to control his reaction, he flinched. Had the incident been part of his father's disgrace? Did the custom explain why the same family had ruled the Defenders for several generations? Were any rivals identified and bonded with unsuitable mates so they were banished when the bondings failed?

The Swordmaster half-rose. "Go to your suite. Sleep well. In three days the gong will summon the patrols for the Ingathering. You will meet your final bondmate."

Alric backed to the door. He didn't trust the older man not to throw the knife he held. For an instant he studied the lines of fire on the Swordmaster's skin. Dark, turgid and touched with evil. The state of the leader's lines meant he had turned toward the ways of darkness. If challenged, could he be defeated?

As he stepped into the hall, tension shot along his spine. His chest felt as though iron bands circled his ribs. Two men he wished to avoid approached. Robec, the leader's son and Petan, the bully, sauntered along the corridor. Alric glanced at their arms. Both remained unbonded. He'd heard about Petan's ill-fortune with his bondmates. Robec had never been chosen. Why?

"Country boy," Petan drawled. "No bracelet?"

The band around Alric's chest prevented him from drawing a deep breath. "Just as you have none. At least my former mates are alive. Didn't both of yours suffer tragic accidents?"

Anger flashed in the beefy man's dark eyes. "Stupid gits. Last one tried to take a duel I'd marked as mine."

Had Petan taken the young woman's life rather than the killer being the man she'd fought? Petan had killed the fighter so there was no one to say what had happened.

Alric turned to Robec. "Do you have taunts to add?"

A flash of color stained Robec's face. During their training years, he had been Alric's closest rival for honors. Alric had usually emerged the winner. He believed his rival saw the lines of fire though he failed to use them. Was the reason personal? Did Robec see the dark lines of his father and his friend and refuse to believe what they meant?

When he refused the Swordmaster's choice, which of his rivals would issue the challenge? He knew Robec's style. Petan had been a year ahead of him so he and Alric had never dueled.

Robec cleared his throat. "Successful trip?"

"Five duels. No deaths. I've only one on my

record." He grinned. "There was a sixth duel but no Justicar was present. Was with a desert rider. He was good but not good enough."

"Should have killed the scum." Petan clamped Robec's arm. "Come on. We're due at the Women's Quarters. Kalia's waiting."

"You're right." Robec's voice sounded devoid of emotion. "She doesn't like to wait for anyone."

Alric's hands fisted. Who had given Petan permission to enter the area where many of the unbonded women and a few of the bonded ones had chambers? Robec's mother and sisters stayed there. Petan had no female kin living in the Hall. Was this another exception to the rule?

He hurried along the corridor to the south wing of the sprawling building. In his suite he opened windows to clear out the stale air. He set his pack on the bed and removed dirty clothes. He carried them to the baths and dumped them in the hampers. Some would be washed and mended. Others turned to rags. The soft buckskin trousers would be cleaned and brushed.

He stripped and stepped into the hot pool. After a quick scrub of his body and his hair, he plunged into the warm rinsing pool. After drying and donning a change of clothes taken from the shelves, he combed and braided his hair, binding the ends with a strip of leather.

Food next. He'd missed the nooning. His stomach growled. He headed to the refectory. Taking a wooden tray and mug he moved along the line selecting a hearty meal of sliced beef, tubers and fresh greens.

At the end of the line he filled two mugs with citren and scanned the tables. No members of his patrol were to be seen. His gaze locked with one belonging to a young woman with touches of fire in her brown hair. Time fled. The degree of connection nearly caused him to drop the tray. She was perfect. Who was she? He had to learn her name.

When she lowered her gaze he noticed her companions. Was she Robec's sister or his chosen bondmate? If so, a problem existed. Another thought made him ill. Had she been chosen by the Swordmaster as Petan's third mate?

Alric clutched the tray. He refused to think she had any connection to Petan. The lines of fire on her skin showed the vivid scarlet of health and vitality. Alric walked to a small empty table. He had seen a woman he would gladly choose.

* * *

Kalia watched the stranger walk to an empty table. The few moments when their gazes had meshed filled her with a need she couldn't express. Who was he? The lines of fire on his skin glowed. During the short time she'd felt a connection she wanted to explore, yet she was afraid. He was a Defender, a man who dueled with sword and knife. Just like her father. Did the stranger also revel in causing death? She couldn't live with such a man. Was he the one chosen as her bondmate?

Her hands tightened. Why would the Swordmaster not choose a man she could gladly accept? Though she had mastered the knife and sword skills, she had refused to join a patrol and be forced to duel.

She wanted to explore the tricks she had discovered. Stopping a wound from bleeding, drawing blood away from or to an area of the body where it was needed and how once she had changed a clot to flowing blood, saving a man's life. Her mother had warned her not to tell her father how she used the lines of fire. Only Lasara had known and had also succeeded in halting the flow of blood.

"Dreaming of Ingathering Day?"

With a start her head jerked up to meet Petan's leering stare. His knowing smile raised an anger and fear she dare not express.

"No." She turned to her brother. "Walk me back to the Women's Quarter." Her tolerance for another moment in Petan's company flew like birds migrating in the autumn.

"I'll do the honors," Petan said.

Kalia stared at Robec. The thought of being alone with Petan roiled her stomach. Would her brother agree?

"Not today." Robec rose. "Being alone with my sister would compromise her. I'll see her back. Meet me in the salle. Must practice in case I'm challenged tomorrow."

The burly man ran a finger along Kalia's arm. "Won't be long before we're together."

Her skin prickled. She stared at the lines of fire on her arm. They had faded just like her mothers appeared after a visit to the Swordmaster's suite.

Petan's words chilled her. She watched him swagger away.

Robec rose. "Why were you in a trance earlier?"

"That man." She pointed. "Who is he?"

Robec grasped her arm. "He isn't anyone you want to know."

"Why not?"

"Our father dislikes him. Tried to get him banished on several occasions but couldn't prove he'd done anything wrong."

"Why?"

"Does the Swordmaster need a reason? I'm afraid it's my fault. During our training days, he was the best with sword and knife. Father didn't like me to be second so he set Petan and me against him."

Kalia whirled to face him. "Not fair. I don't like Petan. There's something wrong with his lines of fire."

Robec grasped her shoulders. "Those aren't to be mentioned where someone might hear. Seeing other people's lines is forbidden. Didn't Mother warn you?"

"She did but you and I both see them. Petan's are almost black. I know he's your friend, but open your eyes."

"Kalia, put your dislike aside."

"What do you know?" Her throat tightened and she could barely choke out the words.

He stared at the ground. "Father has promised you to Petan as his third mate."

Her legs buckled. She pressed her hands against the table for support. "I'll refuse."

"Can you? Father will force you. He has his plans for us. When I'm the next Swordmaster, Petan

Lines of Fire

will be my Right Hand. Lasara's bondmate will be my Left."

Kalia pushed away from the table. "And you're happy with the plans?"

"Why wouldn't I be?"

She rubbed her arms. "What you've been promised goes against tradition. I found some forgotten records from the early days. The best dueler among the Defenders is to be the next leader. Instead of a duel where Father allows you to win, you should have a real challenge. Petan should be banished. He's already killed two bondmates." Though angry her voice barely rose above a whisper.

"You don't know that's what happened."

"And you don't know if what he reported was true. There were no witnesses."

Kalia ran from the refectory and dashed down the hall. Robec's friend was a leech just like Father. Petan had sucked vitality from her lines. He had done the same to the two women chosen as his mates. Though the first had died after falling into an icy stream and the other had been killed during a duel, Kalia knew he had been the killer. But there was no proof.

"Kalia, wait." Robec called.

She continued her frantic race through the winding corridors of the central area of the Hall until the door of the Women's Quarters appeared. She opened the heavy oak door leaving her brother behind. She wouldn't listen to his attempt to make his friend's case.

She dashed across the large lounge and nearly collided with her mother. The older woman wore the clothes she donned when she went to meet her bondmate. Her lines of fire showed health and vitality but when she returned they would be drained.

"Daughter, what's wrong?"

Kalia grasped her mother's arm. "Don't go. This time he might kill you."

"Roban called for me. My honor is to serve him. He seeks another son should Robec fail. What troubles you? Did you quarrel with your brother?"

Kalia shook her head. "Father intends to bond me to Petan."

Her mother backed away. "He mentioned he had chosen a mate for you. He said the man would be a power among the Defenders. Why are you angry? Your brother trusts this young man."

"He shouldn't." Kalia grimaced. "I don't like him."

"How can your father be wrong? He's clever at choosing those who are heart bound."

"This time he failed. Years ago Father ordered Robec to become Petan's friend. That was before they entered training. Who is Petan? No one knows where he was born."

"Does that matter? He has shown skill with the sword and knife."

"Don't you worry about me? Petan killed two bondmates."

"Rumors spread by men jealous of the favor this young man has found with your father." She reached into her pocket. "Since you are to be bonded, this is for you." She drew out a glittering bracelet.

"Where did you get this? I've never seen

another like it."

"My dearest friend passed it to me before she entered the abyss. Her bondmate was your father's best friend. He fled to the rebels and broke their bond. Your father brought the news to her and offered comfort. She turned away and only spoke to her young children. They were sent to be fostered. There had been a third child who was stolen by his father."

Kalia felt the weight of the bracelet with its links of silver, gold, electrum and copper. She had read of bracelets of other metals in the ancient records but they had been just made from a single metal.

"It's beautiful." She kissed her mother's cheek and prayed the older woman wouldn't be drained to death during her stay with the Swordmaster.

She watched her mother walk to the door. Robec had remained outside. Kalia wondered why her mother stayed in these quarters. Many bonded woman whose mates didn't go on patrol lived with their mates.

A thought occurred. If her mother remained with the Swordmaster she would die. If I am bonded to Petan, so will I. She darted into her sleeping chamber and threw herself on the bed. What am I going to do?

The special knock announced her younger sister. Lasara didn't wait for an invitation. She crossed the room and sat on the edge of the bed. "Are you excited? In three days you will choose your first bondmate."

Kalia wiped her eyes on the blanket. "Excited, no. Scared, yes. I intend to refuse the man Father has chosen for me."

"Why?"

Kalia sat up. "Would you bond with Petan?"

Lasara's eyes widened. "Ugh. Why does Father get to choose?"

"Some plan of his to make sure Robec follows him."

"What will you do if he tries to force a duel?"

"Saddle my bihorn and ride away."

Lasara's shoulders slumped. "Won't you be afraid? You've never been away from the Hall except during the training exercises."

"I will be frightened. Better scared than bonded to a man with tainted lines."

"Where will you go?"

Since she had no real plans she shrugged. "Just away from here."

Lasara stayed for a bit longer. After she left Kalia found the pack she'd used just once when she trained. She'd refused to be part of a patrol and only bonded women were sent with their mates to tour the sectors. She sat on the bed and tried to plan an escape.

Chapter 2

On the second day of his stay in the Defenders Hall, Alric skipped breaking his fast to explore the Archives. He entered the shelf-lined room and lit several lanterns. After studying the labeled shelves, he pulled volumes for the years just before he left the Hall. He had been five so his sibs must have been younger. Each of the hand-written books began with a listing of the names of the members of the patrols, their bondmates and number of children. He couldn't find his father's name. Were the pages missing?

He took later books and scanned the lists for the children sent to be fostered in villages or on farms. He groaned. The listings weren't by name but by sex and no mention was made of their destination. Even if he had searched the day he'd arrived for training, he wouldn't have learned anything.

There had been no time for research in those hectic days. And since joining a patrol he'd been away from the Hall for most of the time. Other things had seemed more important than learning about his siblings. Each round of a sector lasted a year and a patrol moved from sector to sector until all four had been covered before returning to the Hall. During the year of residence in the Hall between patrol assignments, Sando had sent him on special missions. His patrol leader had known of the Swordmaster's animosity.

Alric slammed the last of his chosen volumes shut. He wanted answers. The connection he'd felt to

Jens had been strong. Was the desert rider his brother? Jens had lived in the Hall until he turned three. There'd been a sister but Jens hadn't remembered having one. Was the sister older or younger?

Sadness filled his thoughts. Even after twelve years he missed his father. His memories of the tall man with the haunted green eyes filled his thoughts. He had no memories of anything before reaching the distant village.

The lanterns flickered. He turned a few more pages and knew his search was futile. Children had been sent from the Hall but the lack of any real information stymied him. Did the Swordmaster know? Asking the older man was a dead-end. The leader of the Defenders would never tell.

Alric closed the book. There were no answers here.

One by one he returned the volumes to the shelves, making sure they were placed in the proper order. He selected several more from the years before he had turned five. He wanted to look at the records of his father's service as a Defender. As he read the records he discovered his mother's name. Jenla. Nothing else was noted, not even his birth. His father had been a remarkable dueler. Reading the words of accomplishments brought a warm feeling.

Then he came upon a page covered with ink. Only a single name remained. Alron. Banished.

His stomach growled. He rose and glanced outside. Midday. He returned the books to the shelves and blew out the lanterns. After leaving the Archive he strode to the refectory. He lifted a wooden tray and selected a variety of dishes.

One of his patrol members waved. "Over here," Ganor called.

Alric carried the laden tray to the long table where his patrol sat.

"When did you get in?" his patrol leader asked.

"Last evening. Reported to the Swordmaster, bathed, ate and slept. Spent the morning in the Archives."

Sando leaned forward. "Kept expecting you to join us on the road."

Alric's shoulders slumped. "Had to think."

"No shame the bonding didn't take. She would never have been comfortable as a Defender."

Masine, Sando's bondmate nodded. "Did she find what she wanted?"

Alric grinned. "Her childhood friend waited for her."

The patrol leader's wife clasped his hand. "Never understood why some girls are chosen for our ranks. Can tell during training they won't fit."

Ganor clapped Alric's back. 'Choice is yours this time."

"Perhaps."

"What do you mean?" Sando asked. "Third choice belongs to the man or woman. The Swordmaster must allow you a year to find your mate and a year or more for the deciding on the length of the bond."

Alric finished a banta leg. "The Swordmaster has made a choice for me. I told him I would refuse. He said I couldn't and mentioned some kind of unwritten exception."

Sando propped his elbows on the table. "There is no such rule. Refuse his choice. We'll stand beside you. Our leader has made odd decisions lately. There's been talk." He shrugged. "We'll discuss this at practice. Come to the salle with us."

"Good idea to practice," Ganor said. "Sure to be at least one challenge tomorrow, especially when you've decided to refuse."

Alric nodded. He was sure to be one of the challenged. Who would fight the duel, the woman or a champion she chose? There were few members of the Defenders present in the Hall he couldn't defeat.

A stir at the door drew his attention. Robec entered. For once his shadow wasn't at his side. A young woman ran after him. Unlike the garb usually worn by the women, she wore tight trousers and a vest without a shirt. Her voice rang over the normal buzz of the voices.

"You tell your father I'm the one you choose as your mate or I'll tell him what you've done."

"I've done nothing." Robec shook off her hand. "You're not for me. My father has selected the best dueler among the returning patrols as your bondmate."

"Aren't you the best? Isn't that what you always say? So does Petan. Are you liars?"

"Who is she?" Alric asked.

Sando leaned forward. "No one you want to know. Though her father is the Right Hand, she should have been fostered. She has been chosen twice and both have left the Defenders in disgrace."

Alric frowned. "Then the Swordmaster plans to name her as my chosen." He studied her lines of fire and noted they were the palest he'd ever seen on anyone standing as a Defender.

She reached for Robec again. Her hand rolled down his arm.

He pulled away. "Do not touch me again or I'll see you banished."

Her lines flared brighter. Had Robec's faded when she touched him. But she had no darkness in her lines. This was another puzzle to solve.

Alric finished his meal and went with the members of the patrol to the salle. After drawing stones they divided into two teams for a melee. With practice swords and knives the game began. The blunted blades had colored chalk on all points and along the edges to show where a wound occurred and the severity.

He laughed and allowed his frustration over the futile search of the records and his annoyance with the Swordmaster's attempt to control his bonding and guide his actions. The group melee ended when he took a fatal wound and delivered one to the patrol leader.

Alric leaped to his feet and slapped Sando's back. "Good fight."

"Agreed. I believe you're ready to face any man who challenges you." Sando grinned. "To the baths."

As Alric joined the men and women of the patrol walking from the salle, he noticed Robec and Petan had been among the spectators. Petan's scowl contrasted with the admiration on Robec's face.

He turned to Ganor. "We were watched."

"Looks that way," Alric's friend said. "Maybe scouting the opposition. Neither belongs to a patrol."

"I wonder why?" Alric asked.

Sando moved closer. "No patrol will have Petan in their ranks these days. The deaths of his two bondmates occurred when there was no one to testify as to the cause. The Swordmaster refused to allow the Justicars to examine him. He also refused to risk his heir being injured or defeated in a duel."

"Then I guess Robec won't challenge me."

The older man shrugged. "He might be named as a champion for someone. After the baths, I suggest we exercise our steeds."

"Good thought," Ganor said. "Is Storm Cloud up for a race?"

"He's rested since we returned." Alric followed the men inside, undressed and slid into the hot pool. "You're on for the race."

Sando tossed Alric the soap. "Bothers me that Petan witnessed the melee."

"Why?"

"He'll be the Swordmaster's choice to face you in a challenge," Sando said.

Alric shrugged. His ability to read the lines would help, especially with the sluggish movement he'd seen in the blighted lines of his enemy. As he scrubbed chalk marks from his arms, chest and throat, he wondered if Sando knew anything about his father's banishment and where his sibs had been sent.

He swam to the slide into the rinse pool and listened to his companions discuss the coming meeting of the returned patrols. Of all the members, he was the only one without a bondmate. Some of the men mentioned women they wanted him to meet. He knew who he wanted to choose but he didn't know her name.

How could he learn?

Alric rubbed himself dry. "Who's up for the race?"

Six of the men followed him to the stables.

As he saddled Storm Cloud, the bihorn seemed restless. Alric laughed. "Been resting too long?" He held several apelons on his hand for the steed. "We'll beat them all."

Once the riders lined up outside the gates, Sando raised his hand. "To the first crossroads."

Alric's whoop joined those of his friends. They raced down the road. Not more than fifty yards from the gate Storm Cloud reared. Alric grasped the steed's horns to keep from being thrown. The other riders streaked ahead. Alric dismounted and checked his bihorn's hooves. From one he pulled a wide brass nail.

"Looks like the race is over for us." He grasped the reins and led the limping animal to the gate. Who had done this and why?

***

Kalia helped her mother into bed. The older woman's lines of fire were as pale as the ones Ilna sported most of the time. Only when the other young woman had been with a man did her lines show any vitality. A kiss or a touch seemed to be enough to change them. Was that phenomena related to what happened to the Swordmaster's wife after a stay in his quarters?

"Mama, why do you allow him to do this to you time and time again?" Kalia asked.

The older woman's eyes opened. "A bondmate's duty is to see to her mate's comfort. You will understand once you wear Petan's bracelet."

"I won't." Kalia drew a deep breath. She wouldn't tell her mother how she planned to flee rather than be bonded to him.

"You must. When Robec is named Swordmaster he will need a strong Right Hand. Your father believes Petan will be the one."

Kalia rose. "I won't argue with you today." She walked to the door. 'Rest and regain your strength. I'll send someone with broth, citren and kafa." How long would the recovery take this time? After her mother's last visit to her mate, a week had passed before her mother's lines had brightened.

Her hands tightened into fists. Tomorrow was the day of choosing. On the day when the returning patrols celebrated Ingathering, her father would allow Petan to name her as his bondmate. If she must duel, she would. Better to die beneath the blade than be milked of her essence by a man she believed was evil.

Kalia left the area where the women who either weren't bonded or didn't live with their bondmates stayed. She raced along the corridors until she reached her father's office. She tapped on the door and wished for once he would listen. Could she convince the Swordmaster that a bonding with Petan would mean her death? Did her father care?

Petan was a leech. Just the other day his touch on her arm had drained some of her lines of fire. She shuddered. Just like her father changed her mother's lines.

An image of the pale wiggling creatures used by the Healers to clean wounds made her stomach lurch. Rather than essence, the creatures removed dead tissue from wounds.

Thankfully she had pulled free from Petan before he had stolen more than she could spare. During her mother's days with the Swordmaster, her father stopped before depletion occurred. Petan wouldn't. He was greedy. The deaths of his former bondmates told her the truth of his nature.

She knocked louder.

When her father called, Kalia stepped inside and paused before the desk. "I have something to say."

The Swordmaster's mouth curved into a smile. His eyes remained cold as bits of green glass. "I'm sure you've heard what will happen tomorrow. Secrets are few in the Hall. As you suspect, Petan will claim you as his mate."

Kalia stared at her father. She dare not cave to his demands. "I heard but I didn't believe you would do this to me. I will refuse." A shudder shook her body. She forced the words past her tight throat muscles a second time. "I will refuse."

He rose and pressed his hands against the mahogany desk top. "You will do as I command. You are my daughter. Your bondmate will stand as your brothers' Right Hand when he takes my place as leader."

Kalia quieted her desire to attack her father. She needed to remain calm. "Find another mate for Petan. He has killed his last two mates. Will you see me become the third?"

With a quickness she hadn't expected he moved around the desk. "Those foolish young women refused to give him what he needs. You are stronger and were bred to do this, just as your mother was."

So he knew of Petan's tainted lines. Kalia drew a deep breath. Her fisted hands hung at her sides. "I will refuse. That is my right. I've read the archived records. From the first days when our people came to this land, mates were to be freely chosen." She backed toward the door.

"You will obey." He stalked toward her.

"I would rather die by the sword."

She didn't expect his reaction. Like a striking snake his hand lashed out. The blow landed on her face hard enough to send her back until she collided with the door.

"Do not defy me." He fisted his hands. "I will beat you senseless but you will accept Petan. Go to your chamber and prepare for tomorrow. Do you understand?"

Kalia reached behind her for the latch. She dare not turn her back to him. With her cheek aching from the blow she ran along the hall toward the sanctuary of her chamber. Time to put her plan of last resort into action. Determination stiffened her spine, Tomorrow she would defy her father.

She chose clothes and stowed them in the pack she'd used several years before during the training exercise. She added a comb, soap, several towels and some ties for her braid. She selected a chain and slipped the bonding bracelet her mother had given her onto the chain and tucked it beneath her shirt.

On the bed she laid the clothes she would wear in the morning. Lifting the pack, she crept from the chamber and entered the bathing room. There, she used a door to reach a seldom used corridor.

When she reached a door leading into the courtyard she raised the bar and peered into the empty forecourt. After racing across the flagstones she ducked into the stable and went to her bihorn's stall and slipped inside. She hung the pack on a hook where the stablemen wouldn't notice. She stroked Mist's coat.

"Tomorrow," she whispered. Though she had no clear destination other than being beyond her father's reach she would escape. With luck, she could join the rebels and share her knowledge of the past and her discoveries of using the lines to heal.

A snorting bihorn startled her. She peered over the stall's gate and saw a man leading a limping steed. As he drew closer her breath caught. He was the man whose gaze had promised much. She stepped back and bumped into the wall with a thud.

"Who's there?" he asked. "Planning to attack?"

Kalia opened the gate and stepped outside. "Don't hurt me."

"Who are you?"

"Kalia. And you." His presence rattled her and she couldn't remember his name if she had ever heard it. Their gazes met. His lines of fire flared.

"Alric. What are you doing here?"

The hint of suspicion in his voice produced a chill. "My bihorn. Nothing else."

His eyes narrowed. "Are you in trouble?" He touched her hand.

The fingertips graced her skin and brought a promise of safety. Could she believe him? She needed to take control. "Why would you think someone planned to attack you?"

"There are some in the Hall who don't like me." He held out his other hand. "Found this in Storm Cloud's hoof. Bothers me."

She saw a large brass nail. "Why?"

"Went to race some of my patrol. My steed refused the challenge. Found this. Good way to bring me back early and with no one to cover my back."

Kalia froze. She glanced around. Had Petan or her brother suspected her plan to run? Would she be discovered with this man who interested her? Fear caused her to tremble.

His hold on her hand tightened. "What's wrong?"

"We shouldn't be here alone." Could she trust him? Her thoughts bounced from yes to no and back. The desire to believe he would help her strengthened. She thought of what Robec had told her. The Swordmaster wanted a reason to banish Alric. He was as out of favor as she would be when she refused the bond with Petan.

Drawing a deep breath, she began. "I have to flee. My father has chosen a man as my bondmate I won't accept." She touched her cheek where her father's blow had landed.

He slid a finger over the tender area. "Who did this?"

"Does it matter?"

"You have the right of refusal."

As she stared at Alric, his fingers glowed scarlet. Her cheeks burned. Gradually the sensation faded and the pain vanished. What had happened? Could he use the lines to heal?

She stepped back. "Yes, I can refuse but how can I face Petan in a duel? I have no experience with dueling. I have no one to act as my champion."

"Why can't you duel? Surely you have passed the training exercises."

"I learned the forms and practiced dueling but I find no pleasure in fighting."

"Why weren't you fostered to one of the villages? A Defender has to enjoy dancing with the sword and knife."

"I'm the Swordmaster's daughter. Rules are different for his children. My father plans to mate me with the man who will stand as Robec's Right Hand."

Alric shook his head. "Robec may not be the next Swordmaster. Someone could challenge your father and win. Do you think Petan will be satisfied to be just one of the Seconds?"

Kalia frowned. He had just spoken to one of her fears. "Do you understand what happens in the Hall and has for generations?"

"Tell me."

"My father, his father and before him for three generations have been the leaders of the Defenders. So it will be when my father steps aside."

Alric shook his head. "How can that be? Robec has never been part of a patrol. I know your father was when he was younger. Robec has never had a bondmate. He has never fought a duel except in practice."

"I know about the rules that govern our Guild after they used the mists to enter this land. I've read the ancient records. Those ways have ended and there are new ones." Her hands shook and she clasped them together.

Alric touched her arm. Where his skin brushed hers their lines met.

She gasped. "Do you see what's happening?"

He nodded. "When I duel I watch my opponent's lines. Knowing where the lines move allows me to win without killing my opponent. You could do the same."

Kalia shook her head. "I won't use the lines to fight unless I have no choice. I can stop bleeding and sometimes do what you did to my cheek. Once I cleared a blood clot by manipulating the lines. If permission had been granted I would have joined the Healers."

"I don't think you could learn from the Healers. They have different talents. You are a Defender."

"I will escape before I'm bonded to a man with lines so dark they suck vitality from a bondmate."

"Are you sure that's what happens?"

"My father does. I've seen my mother's lines when she returns from a visit. I'm sure Petan did the same thing to his mates."

"I've seen the lines of Petan and the Swordmaster and believe they are unnatural. What do you know about your mother's?"

Kalia drew a deep breath. "When she leaves to stay with him, her lines are as bright as mine. When she returns they're pale, almost as faded as the lines of the dying. Will you help me escape before I become Petan's victim?"

"If you won't fight I'll be your champion." He raised her hand to his lips.

The wave of heat flowing from his mouth stormed her body and frightened her. How could she accept his offer? As her champion, if he won, the patrols would demand their bonding for the trial period. She dare not think of what her father would do to him during that time.

"Kalia! What is going on here? How could you ignore my warnings?" Robec tramped toward them.

She pulled her hand free. "Nothing has happened."

Her brother faced Alric. "You will be challenged and banished for taking liberties with my sister."

Kalia froze. What would happen if Alric and Robec fought? Robec would lose and their father would explode in fury. "He did nothing other than listen to me. That's more than you, mother or father have done." She turned and ran. The need to escape the Hall escalated.

Chapter 3

Alric watched Kalia's rapid retreat. He knew what he must do. Win or lose, he had to offer to be her champion and face Petan in the dueling circle. To challenge Robec was impossible. The Swordmaster wouldn't allow his son to fight when he could lose. Alric led Storm Cloud to his stall. He turned and saw that the other man remained.

Would Robec challenge him now? A duel outside the salle would be grounds for banishment. Surely Robec knew but he also knew the rules were different for him. As the Swordmaster's son he was protected. If they fought no matter who won, Alric knew he would lose. The promise he'd made to his father flashed in his thoughts.

"You've done a forbidden thing," Robec said. "How did you manage the meeting? Kalia is promised."

Alric leaned against the rough wood of the stall gate. "Are you sure I arranged this? I was out for a race with friends. My steed went lame. I returned and found your sister here."

"You touched her."

"I did. Does the reason matter? Are you one who follows unwritten rules, ones your father invented?"

Robec rose on his toes. "He is the Swordmaster. He has the right to guide the Defenders."

Alric drew a deep breath laden with the aromas of the stable and a sharp scent he didn't recognize. "I won't argue with you about your father. Just this. I encountered your sister by accident, not for a tryst. Why are you here?"

Robec's gaze darted from side to side. "I came because someone told me Kalia was meeting someone here. You said your bihorn went lame. Have you proof?"

Alric opened his hand to show the wicked nail. "You can check his hoof and see how the tissue is torn. Your sister was hiding in one of the stalls. She's afraid of someone or something."

"Of being forced into a bonding with you." Robec said.

Alric laughed. "Not with me. With your father's choice. Have you listened when she spoke of that?"

"What she wants doesn't matter. The Swordmaster's orders will be obeyed." Robec's hand hovered over the hilt of his sword.

Alric's eyes narrowed. Was Robec trapped in a web his father had spun? The lines on his skin flowed in an erratic pattern as though he struggled for control.

"Why would he force a bond between your sister and a man she fears? Makes no sense unless he's buying loyalty."

"Petan is heart bound to her. He told me that was why his other bonds failed. The women guarded their hearts. My father says every man is entitled to bond with the woman they love that deeply."

"But your sister doesn't feel about him that way," Alric said.

"Women don't matter. What the Swordmaster orders is always right."

"Well now, what do we have here?" Petan swaggered into view. "Are you fighting with the Swordmaster's son?" He grasped Robec's arm.

Alric watched the lines on both men's skin. Robec's changed to match Petan's. What had happened? He turned to leave.

"You're not going anywhere," Petan said.

Robec looked at his friend. "He was here with your chosen."

Petan's laughter held a cruel edge. "Then we have him. Your father will be happy." Petan's feral grin sent a chill climbing Alric's spine.

"What do you mean?" Robec asked.

"We have him here. Toss his body with my bihorn. Smell of blood sends the beast into a stomping frenzy. Like magic, no one will know how he died."

Robec shook his head. "I want to challenge him tomorrow. He's said to be the best. When I beat him no one will dispute my right to follow my father."

"The Swordmaster won't like that. If you must duel I'll be your opponent. If he's gone I am the best. You beat me and you'll show everyone how good you are. Your father has agreed."

Some quality in Petan's voice made the words sound false. Was the bully's plan different from the Swordmaster's? Alric drew a deep breath and prepared to defend himself.

The clatter of hooves on the flagstones of the courtyard caused Petan and Robec to step back. Sando and Ganor strolled inside leading their steeds.

Sando clapped Alric's shoulder. "What happened? Why did you quit the race? Storm Cloud always wins."

Alric produced the nail. "Found this pounded into his hoof. Do you have any of that goo that farmer gave you?"

"A full jar. Remind me to give the Healers a sample." Sando walked away.

Ganor leaned against a stall. "Enjoying the company?"

"Heard some interesting things." Alric grinned at Robec's red face.

A glaring Petan grasped Robec's arm. "We need to go. Your father sent me to find you."

"Just a minute." Robec turned to Alric. "No one should treat a prime steed like yours was." He pointed to the nail. "I had nothing to do with that."

Petan halted. "Could be he did it himself. Maybe he found a way to arrange a private meeting. Bet he knows Kalia comes to visit her bihorn and tried to persuade her to run to the rebels with him." He stalked back. "Kalia's mine."

"Only if she chooses you."

Petan laughed. "She has no choice. The Swordmaster promised her to me." He strutted away. "You have no say in any bonding. Ilna will be yours." He laughed. "She is a woman of fire and passion."

Robec grasped his friend's arm. "What are you talking about? Ilna will be furious."

"Won't matter."

"How did you learn?"

"The Swordmaster tells me things. If you spent time with him instead of in the training center you would know." Laughter trailed after him. "Have fun tomorrow, Alric."

Alric watched the pair until they vanished. Sando returned with the salve. After cleaning and treating Storm Cloud's hoof, Alric joined his friends. "That was an interesting moment."

"Very." Sando cuffed Alric's shoulder. "Until you retire for the night, stick with us. Don't trust that pair."

"Robec isn't so bad when he doesn't let his father and Petan rule his life." Alric lowered his voice. "I'll refuse the choice made for me and duel with her champion. I will fight for a woman who told me she must accept a man she refuses to choose. She fears Petan. I don't blame her."

Ganor shook his head. "Do you really think this is the time to challenge the Swordmaster?"

"I won't challenge him tomorrow, just the bonds he chooses to force. Kalia will have her choice, not her father's. Besides I can't run. Storm Cloud needs time to heal."

"You could take another mount."

"I won't leave him. He's worth too much."

Sando led his own bihorn into a stall. "Wait to see what tomorrow brings before you act."

Alric nodded. "If I can."

* * *

On Ingathering Day at dawn, Alric joined the men of his patrol in the bathing room. Laughter and chatter filtered over the wall from the women's side. After the morning meal, a gong would summon the four returned patrols and the Defenders who remained in the

Hall. They would march to the salle.

Bathing finished, Alric walked with his patrol to the refectory. They filled one of the long tables. Today the crowded room buzzed with speculation and hope. Alric believed he would be challenged so he chose his meal with care. Eggs, but no sausages or fried meat. Toasted bread and multi-grain cooked porridge. He took two mugs of citren. As he joined his friends his thoughts turned to the Swordmaster's older daughter. Why did the man want his daughter to bond with Petan?

She didn't like her father's choice. Alric had sensed fear in her voice when she'd spoken of the selection.

Robec and Petan entered. The beefy Petan carried a tray laden with food to one of the small tables. Alric grinned. With such a heavy meal the man would be sluggish if he elected to duel.

Sando clapped Alric's shoulder. "We'll stand beside you in your refusal. So will Elgrin's patrol. The other two are undecided but some of their members don't like what the Swordmaster plans."

Alric nodded. "Thank Elgrin."

"Will do." Sando rose and walked to another of the long tables.

Alric ate his light breakfast. He savored the tart flavor of the citren.

A gong sounded.

Alric walked with his patrol to the salle. When classes were in progress, the large practice area with a sand-covered floor had room for three dueling circles. Sunlight streamed through the glass ceiling panels. A scattering of people sat on the benches along one wall.

As Alric's patrol took their place on the arena floor more people entered and slid into the stands. Women eligible for bonding stood against the wall separating the stands from the salle floor.

The Swordmaster strutted into the arena. His Right and Left Hands followed three steps behind. Alric studied the lines of the three men. Only those of the Swordmaster bore a dark red shade reminding him of dried blood. Could the leader of the Defenders lines grow any darker? Was this condition a disease? If so, was there a cure?

The Swordmaster mounted the raised platform facing the seats. His Seconds took places on either side of the steps.

"Welcome to this year's Ingathering of the returning patrols." His deep voice halted the chatter from the attendees. "Begin the reports."

One by one, the patrol leaders joined him to speak of the important events they had discovered during their four years away from the Hall.

When Sando told of Alric's duel with the desert rider, cheers arose. The leader scowled.

Once the four reports ended, the Swordmaster cleared his throat. "The award this Ingathering Day for the most successful duels goes to Alric. Seven duels and no deaths. In the four years of his tour he has had one death and that was justified."

Alric left his patrol and approached the platform. He caught the bag of coins tossed to him. Other awards were given.

Once the applause ended the Swordmaster raised his hands. "Come forward those who wish to declare their bonds as permanent."

Four couples approached the platform.

"Do you swear this is a heart bond?"

"Yes,"

"Then until death draws you across the abyss you will cherish and honor each other."

"We will."

"Dismissed."

The Left Hand unrolled a scroll and handed it to the leader. "The following pairs have declared they will enter a trial bonding period." He read the names.

A dozen couples exchanged the brass bracelets. They swore to attempt to form a permanent bond. Alric wondered how many of them had chosen each other.

The Swordmaster dismissed them. He raised his hand. "Our champion dueler has twice chosen and twice the bonding has failed. I name Ilna as his third mate."

Alric crossed to the platform. "Since this is my third attempt, the choice is mine. I did not choose the failed bondmates but accepted the ones chosen for me. I do not accept this mate. The third choice is mine. According to the rules I have a year to find a mate. If I fail, I will leave the Defenders."

"You can't do this," Ilna screamed. She faced the Swordmaster. "You promised me the best dueler as my mate. You said he couldn't refuse. I demand a duel."

The leader raised his hand. "Alric, do as I command."

Shouts came from the patrols and the stands. "Alric is right. The choice is his."

Ilna whirled. "Then a duel is called for I have been insulted. Robec will be my champion. I haven't the skill to face the best dueler of the Defenders."

The Swordmaster's lines of fire grew as dark as a liver removed from an animal during butchering. His face blanched.

Robec stepped forward. "I accept the request by Ilna to be her champion. Though I will fight for her I will not bond with her."

"As is right." The Justicar rose from his seat. "Since she named you, you are not obligated to bond with her should you lose."

The Swordmaster lowered his hands. "When the choosing ends, the duel will be fought." He smiled. "My older daughter has been of bonding age for several years and hasn't made a choice. I was approached by a man I believe will suit her perfectly. Petan, name your bondmate."

"Kalia."

Alric watched Kalia leave the line of young woman who remained against the wall of the stands. "As is my right, I refuse."

The Swordmaster's face blazed red. "As your father I forbid you to refuse."

"The right is mine. I have no desire to be joined to a man I don't like or trust."

Alric admired the bravery of her defiance. Could she prevail?

"Then I challenge you and any man fool enough to champion you." Petan grinned. "Will you stand in the circle against me?"

"You know I've never dueled except in

practice."

"Then you have no choice." He dangled a bronze bracelet from one finger. "Come, Kalia, admit you are mine. Don't be a fool."

Alric stepped forward. "I'll champion her." The Swordmaster's expression made Alric wonder if he'd stepped into a trap.

The older man laughed. "Then you will face them both in a single duel." He beckoned to his Seconds. "Prepare the largest circle."

* * *

Anger rolled through Kalia's thoughts. Blood pounded in her veins. Her father had done this. Did he really think she would agree to bond with a bully who bore the touch of evil in his lines of fire?

Her thoughts returned to her encounter in the stable with Alric. The warmth of his touch had brought comfort and a yearning for something she couldn't name. Still, the behavior of their lines had frightened her. If she and Alric went beyond touches, would his lines become as dark as her father's? During their meeting, Alric had promised to help her. Would he win against Petan who would never play fair?

Kalia drew a shuddering breath. She would run. Mist was fast. She edged away. A hand clamped on her arm.

"You will obey."

As she opened her mouth to protest no words formed. What was happening?

The Swordmaster turned to face his Left Hand.

"Since my daughter and Lagan's are involved in this duel, you will act as judge."

Sando's patrol remained on the sand. One of the men took Alric's vest and shirt. Alric pulled a chain over his neck and handed it to Sando.

Kalia stared. Alric's broad chest and his honed muscles brought an urge to touch his tanned skin. A line of rich auburn hair led from his chest to the top of his trousers. Beside him her brother looked like a boy. Petan's chest and back made her think of a grizzle.

Her attention turned to the chain Sando held. Sunlight glittered on metal. Was that a bonding bracelet like the one her mother had given her, the one belonging to a dead woman? As Sando's patrol walked to stand around the circle, Kalia tried to pull free of her father's tight grip.

His fingers dug into her arms. "You will sit below me and see what you have wrought. Your only brother faces death. If he dies I will break my bond to your mother and find a younger woman to give me a heir. By your doing you have set Robec's enemy as his opponent." He released his hold and pushed her toward the stands.

A dozen things she wanted to say bubbled toward the surface. As she was about to speak he clasped her shoulders. All words fled. He shoved her onto the bench below his elevated chair. Kalia stared at the dueling circle. What happened when her father touched her? Why couldn't she speak? Next time she would watch his lines and hers. If she could.

The pointed toe of her father's boot touched her back. Would he kick her if Robec fell?

Kalia pressed her hands against the top of the low wall. Alric stood tall and faced his opponent. From the gathered watchers she heard wagers being placed. To her surprise, though he faced two men, Alric was favored to win. How was that possible?

The Left Hand and the Justicar examined the blades of the men. The Justicar wiped Petan's sword and knife with a wet cloth and dried them. What had he removed? Had Petan poisoned his weapons?

"Begin," the Left Hand called.

Petan and her brother charged toward Alric. For the match, the blades weren't the practice ones with the cutting surfaces colored with chalk to mark the injuries. The swords glinted in the light from the skylight overhead.

"To the death," Petan cried.

"To defeat," Alric responded.

Kalia's hands tightened on the railing. Was this a death match? Her father's laughter spoke of his approval of that outcome.

"Defeat," the Swordmaster shouted. He laughed. "First blood goes to Petan. Robec, step aside and allow a superior man to end the duel."

With a flurry or strokes Alric drove his opponents toward the edge of the circle. Kalia half-rose. She wanted to cheer when she saw the sluggish lines on Petan's skin. Surely Alric used them to gauge his opponents' actions.

The movement of the swords mesmerized her. She closed her eyes for a moment.

"No." Her father's cry drew her attention back to the circle in time to see Petan slash Robec's thigh.

Blood spurted from the wound.

"Time," the Justicar called.

Her father's scream of denial hurt Kalia's ears. She jumped to her feet and scurried toward the entrance to the salle floor. Would she be in time to stop her brother's loss of blood?

Alric dropped his sword and knife and sprinted toward Robec. Kalia's eyes widened when he clamped a hand on her brother's thigh. The bleeding stopped. For a moment his lines flickered before steadying.

A scream of warning rose from her throat. She shrieked but didn't think Alric heard her over the noisy chaos. The Healer and several others made their way from the stands. Did anyone see Petan running toward the man kneeling over Robec and halting the fountain of blood?

"No," she bellowed.

Too late.

Alric raised his head and twisted his body away from the descending blade. He failed. The point missed his back but the razor edge sliced a line across his back and arm.

"Foul." The cry rose from the stands.

The Justicar turned. Several members of Alric's patrol grabbed Petan and bound his arms behind his back. Cries from the stands condemned Petan. The sound roared like the whirling winds of summer.

The Swordmaster raised his hands. "Silence. I will judge the matter. Who can say if Petan or Alric injured my only son?"

Kalia's hands clenched. Would he find a way to place the blame on Alric?

The Left Hand strode to the Swordmaster. "I will testify. Petan cut Robec when there was no reason to turn his sword in that direction."

"Truth," the Justicar said. "The Left Hand says exactly what I witnessed."

"Perhaps your gazes shifted for a moment and you missed what I saw," the Swordmaster said.

"Petan, did you cut Robec?" the Justicar asked.

"Yes."

"Truth. Was it deliberate?"

Petan pressed his lips in a firm line.

Kalia clenched her hands. His silence condemns him. What would happen now?

Chanting rose from the crowd. "Cheat. Petan is a cheat. Banish him. Banish Petan now." The shouts roared like a fire at the peak.

The cries thundered in Kalia's ears. She found her way through the number of men and women gathered around the fallen. What would her father do? Would he defy the rest of the Defenders?

His words startled her. "Petan, you have forfeited your position as a Defender. Be gone. You have two hours before you will be hunted."

Chapter 4

Though Alric tried to avoid the descending blade, he failed. His roll prevented a death blow. Excruciating pain followed the slice of the sword along his back and left arm. Would the wound cripple him and force him to leave the Defenders? Anger rose with the pain. How dare Petan attack from behind?

Alric collapsed atop Robec and felt the warm stickiness of fresh blood. Sliding his hand along his companion's leg he realized the flow was his own. He rolled to the sand so the Healers could work on the Swordmaster's son.

Angry shouts chanted words he strained to hear. "Banish him." Over and over the words filled his head. Why did they want to send him away? He wasn't the coward who had struck from behind. He had sped to Robec's side to save him from crossing the abyss against his choice. Robec's friend had been the one to strike the blow.

Alric heard a man's voice. "Damn, the bleeding won't stop."

"Robec?"

"No. Whatever you did stopped the flow from his wound. It's your injury that's the problem."

"Let me," a soft voice said.

Alric felt fingers move slowly along his back. The warmth of the touch told him who was there. He turned his head. "I'm sorry I failed to free you."

"But you did. Petan dishonored his sword and

knife. He's gone," Kalia whispered.

Her touch vanished but he savored her words. He hadn't been sent away in disgrace. He remained a Defender.

Chills shook his body. Shock, he thought. It had happened to him once before after an injury. "Healer, how bad is my injury?"

"Bad enough to need stitching. Imagine you'll be a guest in the Infirmary for a week or so."

Alric shook his head. "Don't have time for that."

The Healer chuckled. "Let me wrap your arm and back. Good thing you moved or the blade would have gone into your heart." He daubed something on the skin. "This will numb the area."

The pain receded. Alric drew a breath. "Thanks."

"How did that woman stop the bleeding?"

"Defender's secret."

"Then I won't pry but sure would like to learn how." The Healer sighed. "Would help when we need to cut people to heal them."

Sando knelt beside Alric. "You all right?"

"Been better."

"Put yourself in a pickle."

"How so?"

Sando chuckled. "Saved the Swordmaster's son. Revealed an interesting talent to everyone. Got rid of your leader's favorite. Coward came after you. All four patrols demanded Petan's banishment."

"Did the Swordmaster agree?" Alric moved his head and felt no pain. Whatever the Healer had rubbed on his skin had worked.

"What could he do?" Sando lowered his voice. "He tried to blame you but the Justicar and the Left Hand exposed the lie. The four patrols have demanded you and Kalia be bonded."

"Only if she chooses."

"Young woman's skittish. You'll have time to consider what to do. You and Robec are off to Healers Hall. Litters are on the way."

"I'm not that badly off," Alric said.

Sando laughed. "Prove it."

Alric pressed his hands on the gritty sand. A jolt of pain nearly made him surrender to darkness. He couldn't rise to his knees.

The Healer tsked. "Do all Defenders believe they're indestructible?"

"This one always does." Sando brushed Alric's hair. "First time he's been hurt bad enough to stop him from the duel. Take your time healing."

"Storm Cloud."

"I'll see to your steed."

"Thanks." Alric forced himself to remain in the present.

Four men arrived with litters. During the transfer from the ground Alric lost his hold on consciousness.

Alien aromas roused him. Herbs and the sharp sting of alk. He tried to turn and yelped. Memories flashed with lightning speed and he realized he was in the Infirmary. "Where?"

"Treating room," a deep voice said. "Drink this and lie still while I apply more numbing salve."

Alric sipped from the bulb and sputtered. "Vile."

"Finish the potion. You need tending and this won't be painless."

Alric felt his back being rubbed. Soon the numbing effect took place. The man with the deep voice barked orders to people Alric couldn't see.

"You were lucky there's no gross muscle damage. Wound isn't as deep as the helpers feared. Take a deep breath. Have to clean the area thoroughly."

Alric felt coldness and smelled the strong aroma of alk. The sting morphed into agony. He lost the battle to remain awake.

Someone's groan woke him. He lay on a soft surface. He heard the groan a second time and realized the noise rumbled from his chest. He tried to roll to his side and bellowed. "Damn."

"Awake now, are you." A young man wearing Healer blue approached the bed. "I'll help you."

"Dry."

"Drinking when sitting is better." The trainee helped Alric to his uninjured side and slid his legs over the edge of the bed.

For a moment, Alric's vision blurred. The young man became two and then four. Alric's stomach lurched and he gulped deep breaths to keep from heaving. The young man changed into two. They swung him onto the bed. Soft pillows cushioned his back.

One of the trainees held a tumbler. "Drink."

Alric gulped a mouthful and nearly spat the liquid. "What kind of poison are you giving me?"

"Salopa. Helps control pain and fever. Finish it

and I'll bring you broth and citren."

"Robec?" Alric asked.

"Here."

The voice came from the next bed. Alric turned his head and studied his companion. Robec's pallor troubled Alric until he saw the lines of fire on the Swordmaster's son's skin. They held a healthy hue.

"How do you feel?" Alric asked.

"Like I've been slammed by a battering ram." Robec cleared his throat. "Kalia came to see us last evening. She said you used the lines to stop my spurting blood."

"I did. Useful skill for a Defender. That's the reason my duels aren't fatal for my opponents. You could learn to do the trick. Don't you see the lines of fire?"

Robec glanced around the room. "Seeing them is a trick I don't admit. The Swordmaster would cast me aside. Seeing the lines is a sign of evil."

"How can you say that?"

Robec lowered his head. "My father taught me to fear such an event. Kalia says he's wrong but she's just a foolish woman. He is the Swordmaster."

"I agree with your sister." Alric winced as he shifted position. "I've read about the old days. One reason our people fled their former land and traveled through the mists to come here was to keep the sorcerers from forcing them to use their talents for evil. Seeing the lines was one of their talents."

"I'll think about what you've said." Robec cleared his throat. "I'm sorry I've been your enemy for all these years."

What brought that on? Was this some kind of trick? "I survived."

"What will you do when you leave the Infirmary?"

"Regain my skill with sword and knife. Seek a bondmate. Maybe go on detached duty."

"Why seek a bondmate? Your patrol leader and the other three have demanded you and Kalia bond."

"And your father?"

Robec laughed. "He agreed. He had to or face challenge after challenge."

Alric frowned. "Why who was ready to issue a challenge against the Swordmaster?" "Who would oppose him?"

"The patrol leaders. Maybe the Left Hand. Father seldom asks for his help these days." Robec yawned. "Why did Petan wound me? He's my friend."

Alric pondered his answer. He had suspicions about the state of Petan's friendship with Robec. Though the other man was his age, Robec seemed younger. Never belonging to a patrol had stunted his growth as a Defender. Alric knew voicing his suspicions would ruin the tentative easing of hostility. Petan had taken a chance. With Robec and Alric dead Petan would easily become the Swordmaster's heir, especially if he bonded with Kalia.

"Could have been the heat of the moment," Alric said. "Some men lose all sense of anything except the duel."

Robec nodded. "Dueling changes Petan. He says killing his opponents makes him feel powerful. All his duels end in death except this last one with you. He says death feeds a man's spirit."

Alric heard slurred edges to Robec's words. A large dose of salopa would do that. What more could he learn?

"How does Kalia feel about bonding with me?"

"She fears bonding with anyone but I'd say she likes you better than Petan. She has never liked him." Robec released a sigh. "She talks about running away. Don't think she will though. She's never been far from the Hall."

"Running would be a rash move." Alric moved his injured arm and groaned.

"She often acts on impulse. She wanted to leave the Defenders and train with the Healers."

"Not if she sees the lines. Why does she fear bonding?"

"Because of what happens with our mother."

Alric closed his eyes. When they'd met in the stable she had spoken of her mother. He wouldn't force Kalia to bond but he wouldn't tell Robec that for fear the Swordmaster would learn. Once he left this place he would seek her and propose a sham bonding. Would give them a year to find solutions.

He must have dozed because the aroma of food roused him. A trainee brought a tray with slices of banta, mashed tubers and a savory sauce as well as other tasty items. He polished the plate and noticed Robec picked at the food.

"At least drink the citren and the soup. You need to replace the blood you lost."

"Why are you so concerned about me? I've been your enemy for years."

Alric set the citren mug on the tray. "My father taught me to look on no man as an enemy except for those who attack from behind. You never have. If Ilna hadn't named you as her champion would you have challenged me?"

"No and I wish my father had been as wise as yours."

After the trays were removed Alric closed his eyes and thought of how to approach Kalia with his plan. At the end of a year if she wanted to run he would help her find a place and continue to the desert to join the riders.

He heard a nasal female voice. "I demand to see Alric. He will be my mate. The Swordmaster promised."

Alric closed his eyes and forced his breathing to slow. He had no desire to speak to Ilna. Swordmaster's promise or not, she had been rejected. If he had to fight another duel to prevent pairing with her, he would.

She stroked her arm. His lines of fire burned. He nearly ended his pretense to knock her away.

"If you refuse to leave I'll call the Senior Medic," a young man said. "Rest is an important part of the healing process."

Alric kept his eyes closed until he was sure she had left. He swung his feet over the edge of the bed and waited a few minutes before standing. Though his arms and back ached, he walked from his bed and around the three others in the room. He had to build his strength and leave the Infirmary. He paused at the door and motioned to the trainee.

The young man walked back. "Do you need

something?"

"Only to leave word about my recent visitor. Do not allow that woman to enter this room. I fought a duel to keep from bonding with her."

"I'll let the others know."

* * *

Kalia knew she should visit her brother and Alric again. She'd gone once and had been thankful Alric had slept. She wanted to avoid the man who had fought her battle and had nearly been killed by treachery. He had granted her the right to choose her bondmate, but the patrols had demanded she and Alric exchange bracelets.

Yesterday, two women from Alric's patrol had visited to welcome her as one of their patrol. Her hands clenched. Why hadn't she told them the truth? She didn't want a bondmate. That wasn't exactly the truth but she couldn't speak to them of her father's threats. There was no need for such a story to spread through the Hall. How could she tell anyone she admired Alric? Her father would find a way to use the demands of the patrol leaders for his own purpose and that was to see Alric banished.

Her other reason scared her. She'd seen the way their lines of fire had moved when they touched. What if Alric could drain her vitality the way her father sapped her mother? A third reason rose. She would be Alric's last chance to remain in the ranks. How could she take the chance of being forced to break the bond?

Her mother appeared at the doorway of Kalia's

chamber. "A trainee has come. Your father demands to see you."

Tension gathered around her. She'd had two days without his demands but she'd known the peace wouldn't last. "I'll go."

"Listen to what he says."

Kalia walked to the door. She touched her cheek. Though no bruises had formed after Alric had touched the spot, the memory of the blow remained. She followed the trainee to the door of the Swordmaster's office. She knocked.

"Enter."

"You wanted to see me." She closed the door and braced for another attack.

"You're prompt." He leaned back in his chair. "Are you pleased with the results of your stubborn resistance?"

She met his gaze. "That I don't have to bond with Petan. Yes."

"Your brother's chances of taking my place as the leader of the Defenders aren't good. He needs a man with Petan's strength to stand at his right hand."

Kalia remained with her back pressed against the door. "I feel sorrow Robec was injured by a man he considered his friend. I'm glad Petan's gone. He tried to kill my brother and take his place with you. If Alric hadn't stopped the bleeding, Petan would have succeeded."

"Matters may not be how they seemed to you."

"What do you mean?"

"How can you be sure Alric's blade wasn't the one to wound Robec?"

"Your Left Hand and the Justicar named Petan and the naming was verified."

He shrugged. "Petan saved Robec's life when he attacked Alric. He acted before that one could smother your brother."

Kalia laughed. "Do you really believe that?"

"Doesn't matter now. You'll be bonded to your brother's enemy. Makes my original plan obsolete but I have another. You will exchange bracelets with him the way the patrol leaders have insisted." He rose and stalked toward her. "At the right moment you will declare the bond broken."

Kalia opened her mouth to protest. He clasped her hand. The words froze on her tongue. "Yes, sir. Is that all?"

"Not quite. If you fail me again, your mother will suffer and may even die. Your brother and sister will be set aside. Do you understand?"

"Yes."

"Dismissed." He released his hold.

Kalia stepped into the corridor. Stunned, she leaned against the wall. Her ability to say anything to contradict him had happened again. She shook her head to dislodge the thoughts that weren't hers. She must escape.

She didn't return to her chamber. She ran outside, across the courtyard and entered the stable. The aromas both pleasant and unpleasant didn't halt her for long. She saddled Mist, retrieved the pack and led her bihorn from the stall.

Her father's plan to banish Alric was wrong. He had saved Robec's life. Would the Swordmaster really harm his bondmate or his children? She couldn't take the chance.

As she led Mist from the stable she glanced toward the gate. Guards stood blocking the entrance. Instead of attempting to leave by the Defenders Gate, she entered the tunnel between the walls leading to the Halls of the other Guilds. She passed the entrance to Healers Hall. Thoughts of Alric and Robec arose. Should she warn her brother? That meant seeing Alric. The connection to him might flare hotter and ruin her chance to escape. Would Robec believe her? Was he too firmly under the Swordmaster's control?

At the opening into Artisans Hall she peered toward the gate. No guards paced around the opening. With a grin she mounted Mist and rode away from the walls. Someone shouted but she paid no heed and pushed her steed into a gallop.

Until dusk she followed the main road. She noticed a side path leading north. She dismounted and saw tracks left by carts. Who had come this way? She decided to chance taking a new direction.

The sky darkened. Stars appeared. She reached a clearing with a fire circle. After gathering wood, she lit the fire. With luck several days would pass before anyone missed her. Maybe not before Alric and Robec were released from the Infirmary.

She toasted bread over the fire and spread soft cheese on the surface. As she put grain in a pan with water to make porridge for the morning meal, she sipped kafa. How long would the food she brought last? She wasn't sure she knew enough about plants to gather them but she had a few coins. If she found a farmer willing to sell or a village with a market, she would spend them.

With a groan she drained the mug, spread her blanket roll and settled down to sleep. A cracking noise startled her. She sat and peered into the dark shadows. Did something move? Her panicked breathing slowed. The thundering beat of her heart ebbed.

Each sound became a wild animal sneaking across the clearing to attack. Wind rustling the leaves became voices whispering secrets. She added wood to the fire, settled again and watched the flames until she slept.

In the morning, groggy from a restless night, she gulped several mugs of kafa and put the rest in her water flask. After drowning the fire she saddled Mist and stowed her gear before continuing along the road. The ruts made by carts seemed fresh. At midday, she saw three wagons parked by the side of the road. Peddlers, she thought and studied the carts. The paint on the sides had faded until she couldn't read the name.

As she rode past a man waved. "Are you the Defender sent to act as our guard? Your partner on the way?"

Kalia halted. "I'm not. I'm on detached duty."

His scruffy beard held streaks of gray and yellow. His clothes bore dust from the road and stains of food.

"You in a rush to reach your destination?" he asked.

"Sort of." Her gaze skittered past him to study the rest of those seated around a small fire. Two women and three men sat on the grass. One of the men looked vaguely familiar but she couldn't recall where she had seen him. Was he a banished Defender? His shirt could have once been green.

"Maybe you could travel with us." The peddler looked at the pack behind Mist's saddle. "For food and coins. All you'd need to do is ride ahead and find camping spots for the night and stop at any farm along the way to see if they were interested in trade."

Kalia thought about the offer and her meager supply of food. "Have you kafa?"

He laughed. "Never travel without the makings."

"Who are you?"

"Name's Hosar. Come and have a bit of nooning with us."

Kalia nodded. "I must think of my duty first." Accepting the offer made sense. Not only would she have a few free meals but she might learn more about the territory ahead.

"In two or three days travel, we'll come to a village. There are half a dozen farms on the way. Aren't very profitable around here. Ground's too rocky but we manage to sell goods made by the Artisan's trainees."

Kalia frowned. Did the Artisans allow their trainees to sell the goods they made? Had she stumbled on a smuggler? She would give the peddler a chance. Hopefully along with the food he provided, she could purchase a few things from the farmers or in a village.

"Will you travel with us?"

"Until my road takes a turn in a different direction."

She accepted a bowl of stew from the woman at

the fire, a mug of kafa and a chunk of dark bread. With her food in hand she sat apart from the others and ate.

When the wagon train moved on, Kalia rode beside the lead one to gauge their speed. Then she rode ahead to find a site for the night.

The journey fell into a routine. Once she stopped at a farm and bought cheese and apelons. Another day, she managed to buy grain and part of a ham. She smiled. She had almost enough food to last for a week or more. From the woman who did most of the cooking, Kalia learned of a few greens and herbs she could pick. Soon she could leave the peddler behind.

What she saw in the small village made her decision easy. One of the men lifted a piece of jewelry from a display in a shabby shop. She witnessed the peddler's thumb touch the scale when weighing kafa beans. She walked to Mist to check her packs, mounted and rode as far and as fast as she could before nightfall.

Chapter 5

Alric held onto the back of a chair with one hand and moved his injured arm in a series of exercises. The pinch and pull of the muscles told him the stitches were due to be removed. He finished the set and prowled the room. Inactivity made him want to scream. Five days had passed since the duel. Five days of boredom. He turned to Robec and saw him raising and lowering his leg.

Alric nodded. "Keep at it." At least his former rival, though not a friend, was no longer an enemy.

Ganor strode inside. "Brought you a present." He dropped several sand-filled leather bags on the bed. "These should keep strengthening your arm and back muscles."

Alric noticed a look of envy on Robec's face. Was he regretting the loss of a friend? Had he realized Petan had done little to earn that title?

"So what's happening outside these walls?" Alric asked.

Ganor glanced toward Robec. "Several assignments in the works. Requests from the Artisans and Justicars."

"That all?"

Robec leaned forward. "Did the Swordmaster really banish Petan?"

"He did. At first he tried to keep him but Petan refused to answer the Justicar's questions. The patrol leaders demanded the banishment be made permanent so the Swordmaster agreed. Didn't matter. Petan vanished. Didn't take his steed. Bihorn savaged a stableman and had to be put down."

"Good riddance," Robec said. "Beast attacked me once."

Alric lifted one of the weights. "Anyone know where Petan went?"

"Who knows," Ganor said.

"And Kalia?" Robec asked.

"Haven't seen her. My mate and Sando's visited her. They enjoyed the meeting. Patrols are insisting on the bonding." He clasped Alric's arm. "Ceremony will take place after you're discharged." He walked to the door. "Have to go. They have me working with the trainees."

Robec reached for his crutches. " I don't like that Petan vanished." He faced Alric. "Watch your back. He doesn't like to lose."

"I remember his rages during the training exercises. Though he was a year ahead of us his expression of anger was violent. Broken practice swords, bruised opponents. Do you know where he's from?"

Robec walked to the door. "He was found near a burned farm by my father's Right Hand. The sole survivor of a rebel attack. He didn't know his name or remember anything about the attack."

"Was he taken to the Nursery?"

"My father brought him into our family." Robec shook his head. "I'd forgotten we were once a family. Petan was afraid of the man who used to be the Left Hand. I was about four or five when he came. A short time later Mother moved to the Women's Quarters. Petan and I stayed with my father, Petan became as close as a brother." He turned away.

Alric heard pain in Robec's voice. He wanted to ask about Petan's lines. Had they been dark even then? Though he and Robec had put their animosity aside the other man remained the Swordmaster's son.

The Senior Healer in charge of their care entered the room. "Time to check your stitches."

Alric lay on his stomach. The Healer and three trainees gathered around his body and removed the dressings.

"As you see, the healing is well advanced," the older man said. "Scissors and forceps. I'll remove the sutures."

"I thought they were to stay in seven to ten days," one of the trainees said. "It's only been five."

"Except for Defenders. They seem to heal faster than others."

"Will you remove mine?" Robec asked.

"I expect to find the same degree of fusion but I want you to use the crutches for another week. You were fortunate the muscle wasn't completely severed."

"Can I leave?" Alric asked.

The Healer laughed. "No reason to keep you." He turned to his trainees. "Another thing about Defenders. They don't like to be confined." He moved to Robec's bed and called for clean instruments. "Light duty for both. No duels for at least ten days."

"Can I ride?" Robec asked.

"No reason you can't but don't be ashamed of asking for help mounting and dismounting."

Within minutes following the departure of the Healers, Alric dressed and pulled on his boots. The moment he found Sando he would ask for a short assignment. Delivering messages or medicines to a distant Healer would allow him to escape the Hall until he sorted through his options. He buckled on his sword and knife.

"Wait for me." Robec swung on his crutches toward the door. "Are you heading to the Women's Quarters?"

"Why?"

"To meet Kalia and set a time for the bonding."

"I stood as her champion to give her a choice, not to force her into a bond."

Robec reached the door. "Won't matter about your decision. You heard what your friend said. The patrol leaders insist on the bonding." Robec caught up. "I wonder why she only visited once."

"Probably because of me." Alric stepped into the courtyard and inhaled a breath of air not flavored by medicinal odors.

"Where are you going?" Robec asked.

Alric paused at the entrance to the tunnel. "To the Hall. After I check on Storm Cloud's injury. Then I'll find Sando and request an assignment. Don't like hanging around the Hall for long."

"I'll come with you and avoid a meeting with my father a bit longer."

Alric strode along the tunnel between the walls toward Defenders Hall. Why did Robec want to avoid his father? Memories arose. Alric brought his father's craggy face into view. He wished he could talk to him and ask for advice on how to avoid being burned by the fires set by the Swordmaster.

Robec's crutches clicked against the flagstones. Alric wondered why the leader's son sought his company. At the tunnel's end he crossed the courtyard to the stable. The sweet aroma of hay clashed with the pungent odors of the stabled animals.

The sound of Robec's crutches stopped. "Mist is gone."

"Who?"

"Kalia's bihorn."

Alric turned. "Does that present a problem?"

"Yes." Robec groaned. "She threatened to run away. Maybe she did. Or my father might have banished her for disobeying him. Maybe Petan stole her."

"Would she go with him?"

"Not willingly." Robec hobbled to the door.

"Wait. We'll check on her together." Coldness filtered into Alric's thoughts. How much control of others did those with the dark lines possess?

Alric checked Storm Cloud's hoof. The gash from the embedded nail had closed and there was no tenderness around the area. He threw a handful of apelons into the manger and strode after Robec. By the time they reached the Swordmaster's office Alric was in the lead.

Robec knocked but didn't wait for a summons. He pushed the door open. "Did you banish Kalia?"

The Swordmaster bolted to his feet. "Why would I do that? She's sulking in her chamber. Been there since the day following the Ingathering. I ordered her to prepare for the bonding but seems she wants neither man."

Alric shrugged. "Her choice. And you haven't seen her since that day."

"Did you check the Women's Quarters?" The Swordmaster resumed his seat.

"Not yet." Robec used his crutches to turn. "Come."

Alric followed and closed the door. "Why didn't you tell him her bihorn is gone?"

"He'd tell us to check the pasture. I'm not up for a walk." Robec led the way along the twisting corridors to the door of the Women's Quarters. He rapped on the oak surface.

A young woman answered. "Robec, I'm so glad you're healed. Father wouldn't allow me to visit." She smiled. "You must be Kalia's bondmate."

"If she will have me."

The young woman grinned. "She will."

She spoke with more confidence than Alric felt. Until Kalia wore his bracelet the bonding could be refused.

Robec tapped her arm. "This is Lasara, my younger sister. She's in her last year of training. Go check Kalia's chamber. We need to speak to her."

"On my way." She dashed away.

Robec turned to Alric. "What will we do if she's gone?"

"Search for her without creating a commotion."

Lasara rushed toward them. "She isn't there. Her pack and some of her clothes are missing. She didn't take the bonding bracelet Sando's mate gave her for you. What will you do?"

"Calm yourself," Robec said.

Alric nodded. "Don't tell anyone, not even your father."

Lasara stared. "Do you think she followed Petan to duel with him? He was a cheat. Ilna said Kalia was angry about his banishment. No one believed her." She gulped a breath and clasped Alric's hand. "You saved my brother. Thank you. Will you also save Kalia?"

"I'll try."

Robec kissed his sister's cheek. "We'll find her." He closed the door. "What now?"

"We look for answers. Could she have gone riding?"

"My father won't let her leave the hall without one of his seconds riding with her."

"Think of where she might go."

They set off to search. By midday they had visited the Archives and spoken to the stablemen. No one had seen her and she hadn't left by the Defender's gate.

Alric turned to Robec. "Rest awhile. I'll check the other gates. If I learn anything I'll let you know. I fear she has run."

"What should I do while I wait?"

"Go to the supplier for food packs. If she's run I'll follow."

"Maybe I should ask my father where Petan would take her."

"Not a good idea."

Alric entered the tunnel. He felt sure Kalia had fled. He emerged near the Healers' gate and checked with the guard there. "Did you see a single Defender leave in the past four days?"

The guard shook his head. "Been no one enter or leave for a week."

"Thanks." Alric returned to the tunnel, he strode to Artisans Hall and paused to ask his question.

"Matter of fact. Three days ago I was returning from a necessary call. Saw the back of a Defender. Figured someone sent a message. Rider galloped away."

"Which direction?"

"North." the man scratched his head. "Don't know why. Aren't many farms or villages on the north road."

"Thank you." Alric turned back. It had to be Kalia. He half ran back to the Defenders Hall.

Once there, he sought Sando. "Put me on detached duty, I need to head out for a few days."

"What about the bonding? Now that you're healed, you must exchange bracelets with Kalia."

Alric looked away. "I need to find her first. She's vanished and I believe she left by the Artisan's gate. Unless you know of someone who was sent that way."

Sando scowled. "Did the Swordmaster send her away?"

"He thinks she's in the Women's Quarters."

"And you don't believe him?"

"Already checked with him. He thinks she's sulking, but even before the duel she wanted to flee."

Sando nodded. "Then detached duty it is. Will you go alone?"

"Robec wants to come."

"Do you trust him?"

"No, but he loves his sister."

The patrol leader walked with Alric to the supplier. "What do you need?"

"Robec said he would come for the food supplies but I could use a new fire starter, some snares and fishing gear. Also maps of the roads north starting at the Artisan's gate."

Sando called the order to the man at the counter. Alric hoisted the small pack and the rolled map. "See you as soon as I can."

"I'll send Ganor and Rila after you. If you take one of the side roads, leave them a sign. Can't afford to take the chance this is a trap."

"Thanks." Alric strode toward the stable. He found Robec seated on a bench at the side of the door.

"Have you any news?" Robec asked.

Alric nodded. "An Artisan saw her leave by their gate heading north. Sando knows where I'm headed. I'll leave now."

"I have the supplies," Robec said. "I want to go. You really shouldn't be alone with Kalia until you exchange bracelets."

"You're welcome to come." Alric grabbed the two packs from the ground beside the bench. "Are you sure you can ride fast and far? What will your father say?"

"I don't care. Help me saddle my steed."

Alric quickly saddled both bihorns. He helped Robec mount and handed up the crutches. "You'll need these." He led both bihorns into the tunnel and walked to the Artisan's gate.

"Why here?" Robec asked.

"This is the road your sister took. We'll need to check to see if she remained on the main road or took a side trail."

"I guess that makes sense."

Alric walked as fast as possible. When would the Swordmaster realize they were gone? He had never allowed Robec to join a patrol. There was bound to be a pursuit. If he and Robec had to leave the main road he would have to leave a sign. Would anyone sent out know the signals?

Once they reached the Artisan's gate Alric mounted and set his bihorn on the road to the north.

When they reached the first crossroad, he dismounted and studied the ground. He saw ruts that meant carts had followed the trail but he also found signs of a racing bihorn. Since there'd been no recent rain to erase the trail, the tracks seemed to have been made several days before.

"We'll go this way." He thought of Kalia and watched his lines of fire move along his hands to point along the trail. Though he wasn't sure what this meant, he had to hope they traveled in the right direction.

"Why take this narrow overgrown trail?" Robec asked.

Alric looked up. "The bihorn tracks appear to be made at the right time and overlay those made by some carts." He stooped and bent a branch of a shrub in a way he knew his patrol members would notice.

"What are you doing?"

"Letting the ones Sando sends after me know

which way we went."

"Why would he do that?"

"For safety."

Robec shook his head. "What about my father's men? Will they know the signs?"

"They might. But it's best to leave our direction. We were both injured and might fall into trouble, especially if Kalia met up with the peddler."

"What if the peddler had a bihorn?"

"The tracks would be beneath those of the carts." Alric wondered if he should tell Robec about the reaction of the lines of fire when he thought about Kalia.

"But the steed could be tied to the cart."

Alric shook his head. "The depth of the tracks indicates a rider. Few peddlers can afford a riding bihorn. Didn't you buy yours?"

"My father gave the animal as a gift."

"Fortunate for you. For my first tour I rode a stack steed and saved to purchase my own. During the return to the Hall we stopped at a farm that breeds bihorns. Storm Cloud's dame had problems. I helped the farmer save her and he gave me a deal on her colt."

For a time they rode in silence. Alric noticed places where the carts had torn brush and weeds from the side of the lane.

Robec drew even. "Do you think my sister has joined the peddlers?"

"She was at least a day behind but unless she finds a different road she will meet them."

"Will they harm her?"

"I don't know." Alric's shoulders slumped. Had

he chosen the right road? Though his lines of fire had indicated this was her route, how could he be sure? Three days was a long lead.

At dusk they came upon a forest glade. The fire circle and the tracks showed the site was well used. Alric dismounted and helped Robec to the ground. Lines of pain etched his face.

"Leg hurting?" Alric asked.

Robec closed his eyes. "My rear, too. I'm not used to riding for hours." He groaned. "Have we really found Kalia's direction?"

"I believe so. I want you to try something. Hold out your hands. Think about her and watch your lines of fire."

"Why?"

"See the direction they point."

For a moment Robec stared at his hands. "I see what you mean. Don't ever tell anyone you can do this."

Alric laughed. "Not until the time is right." He added meat and vegetables to the bubbling pot. Once the stew thickened he dished it into two bowls. "Eat and then sleep."

By the time they spread their blankets, the fire burned low. Alric closed his eyes. Was Kalia safe? How long before they found her?

* * *

A touch on his shoulder followed by a hand pressed to his lips woke Alric. "Who?" he whispered.

"Ganor. Rouse your companion quietly. Bihorns

are saddled. Packs loaded on Storm Cloud. Swordmaster sent Right Hand and selected men after heir. About half hour away. Head through the forest to the main road north. Rila and I will follow and then we'll set our plans to find your mate."

Alric pulled on his boots and donned his sword and knife. After rolling his blanket, he woke Robec. "We need to leave. Your father sent men."

Robec groaned. "Can't. Leg swollen. Find Kalia and send her back alone."

"The pair Sando sent will follow. Are you sure you can't ride?"

"Yes. I'll delay them."

Alric bolted to his feet. He grabbed Storm Cloud's reins and led the bihorn away from the glade. Would Robec manage to delay the searchers? What would he tell them about the reason for choosing this road?

* * *

For two days after leaving the peddler, Kalia rode from dawn to dusk heading through the forest hoping to find the main road north. She believed she was far enough from the Hall to ride through a more settled area. As she rode, she puzzled over the identity of the driver who had seemed familiar. Finally she remembered. He was the Defender who had drilled Petan and Robec before they became trainees. He had also vanished from the Hall but she didn't know why. Had he recognized her?

Near sunset she crossed a rushing stream and

saw a fire pit in a clearing beside what she hoped was the road she sought. After unsaddling Mist she started a fire and stared at the flames. What was she going to do? She had no idea where she was or where she headed. She had planned to join the rebels, but how could she find them?

Why had her father tried to force her into a bond with Petan? Before many days of the bonding would pass, she would have been drained the way her mother was every time she returned from a visit to the Swordmaster.

Petan wouldn't stop before he had completely taken all her vitality. Why couldn't her father see Petan's true nature? Did the dark lines blur his vision? What had caused the taint to invade their lines?

She sent her thoughts into the past. Petan had been the only survivor of a tragedy the year Lasara had been born. The Swordmaster's anger over the birth of a second daughter had been strong. Not long after Petan's arrival, Kalia had been sent to the Women's Quarters with her mother and sister. Had Petan been responsible for the changes? There was no reason to continue the speculation. She would never know.

She left the fire and walked to the stream. She stared into the water and saw several fat chubs swimming near the bank. One of the fish would make a good meal, especially since few rations remained in her pack. After removing her scarf she used the cloth as a net and captured two. She laughed. Two would provide food for tonight and for breaking her fast in the morning. She cleaned the pair at the streamside and carried them to the fire.

With a knife she cut filets and poured oil on a flat metal plate she'd acquired while traveling with the peddlers. She placed it on the grill over the stones forming the sides of the fire pit.

"Enough for two?"

She shrieked and nearly knocked the fish into the fire. When had he arrived? She hadn't heard the bihorn approach.

"Didn't mean to scare you." Alric slid from the saddle.

"How did you find me?"

He unsaddled his steed and removed the packs. "Used the lines of fire and what I learned from an Artisan who saw you ride off. Robec insisted on coming but when a friend warned us about men sent by your father he stayed behind to give me time to follow you."

She used a cloth to pull the plate away from the flames. "Will my father punish him?"

"Why would he harm his heir?"

She stared at her hands. "For now, there's no reason." She turned the fish and returned the plate to the fire.

"Do you fear your father?"

"He has changed since I was a child. He schemes to make everyone act as he wishes. He ordered me to accept the bond with you and break it on his command. If I refuse my mother, sister and brother will die. He wishes to bond with another woman and have only sons."

"There's no guarantee that will happen." Alric opened a pack and filled a pan with water and kafa powder. He placed trail bread and cheese on a cloth. "Why didn't you agree?"

"I won't let him control me."

Alric removed the platter and set the fish on the cloth. "Could you let him think you're doing just that? We would have a year to find a refuge for your family."

"How? He keeps them confined."

"You escaped."

"I know little used ways in and out of the Hall."

He placed a piece of fish on the trail bread and removed the kafa pan. "Before a year ends someone will challenge him. Can you wait that long?"

"If I must. Will you be the one?"

"I hope there will be someone else. I've no desire to become the Swordmaster. I've had no training for leading the Defenders. One of the Seconds or your brother is better suited than I am. Even if your father is defeated his control over Robec could keep him as the leader."

"What do you mean? How does he control my brother?"

"When Robec saw us in the stable and after you ran off, he listened to me. Then Petan arrived and grasped Robec's arm. Your brother spoke in a dull voice and echoed all Petan said. Robec followed Petan's orders."

Her eyes widened. Was that what happened to her when her father touched her hand? She had meant to say one thing. Instead she had repeated his words. What about when Alric touched her? The only change she'd seen was in her lines. But after Alric's touch she had quietly defied her father. Did Alric's touch place her under his control?

She rubbed her arms. "Something odd happened after we touched. What?"

Alric shrugged. "I don't know." He lifted his bread. "Eat before the food grows cold."

For a time they were silent. Kalia drank a mug of kafa and sighed. Nearly three days had passed since her last taste of the sweet yet spicy brew.

Alric finished his share of the food. "Will you listen to what I propose?"

"Yes." If he had a plan to thwart her father she would listen and even follow his suggestions.

"You must return to Defenders Hall with me. We will exchange bracelets."

"But I'm your last chance to remain as a Defender. You know what my father ordered me to do."

"If you don't accept the bond the Swordmaster will make his threat become true. In time we can find a resolution. If we fail I'll make sure you and your family are safe and I'll vanish."

"Where will you go?"

"To the desert riders."

"Why?"

"My last duel before the one here was with a young man I believe is my brother. I never knew I had sibs until my dying father spoke of them. He failed to tell me their names but he asked me to find my brother and sister. The records in the Archives gave no clue to where they had been fostered."

Kalia smiled. Here was a way she could help him. "Did you search the birth records for information?"

"Didn't find records like that. Just lists of bondmates and the number of children they had. In one book, my father's name was scratched out."

"I could look for you and also talk to my mother. She might know something."

"You would do that?"

"Yes."

He leaned forward. "Will you pretend?"

"Yes." She wanted him to touch her again. She wanted to form a permanent bond with him. But the way her lines of fire responded to his frightened her.

Chapter 6

Alric stared at his lines of fire. What had just happened to them? He recalled what she'd said about her father draining her mother's vitality. Had that occurred when they'd touched? His lines remained vivid. So did hers. Something else had just taken place, but what?

He walked to Storm Cloud and stroked the steed's silky coat. For five days he had pushed the bihorn hard. On their return to Defenders Hall he planned to reward the steed.

The sensations storming his body had also happened in the stable when he and Kalia had touched. There had been no change in his lines when he'd touched his other bondmates. Those bonds had lasted for less than four years with nothing beyond casual courtesy. He dare not let the Swordmaster know of the potential of a heart bond. Even Kalia couldn't know. Since she believed her father's threat, she would panic.

With a groan he led his bihorn to the stream. Could he and Kalia convince her father that his plan had worked?

While the bihorn drank Alric struggled to harness his errant thoughts. Wind whispered through the trees. Moonlight shone on the clear water of the stream. He knelt and splashed water on his face. Tonight he had to keep alert. How could he be sure the men the Swordmaster sent after Robec had returned to the Hall? Being caught alone with Kalia, even though they were to be bonded could be looked on as an insult to her.

When he returned to the fire, Kalia cradled a mug in her hands. In the glow of the flames fear flashed in her leaf green eyes. He halted across the pit from her. "I will not harm you."

"What did you do to me?"

"I've tried to understand what happens when we touch but I have no real idea. Happens to me, too. Look at your lines. If anything they're more brilliant. So are mine. When we return to the Hall we must visit the records and read what is written. Maybe we'll find answers there."

She drained the cup. "What if my father learns about the strange reaction? What if it's the same that occurs between him and my mother?"

Alric shook his head. "Unless he can control us with a touch, how can he know what we're doing? I believe what happens with our lines is different from what he and Petan do. Our lines neither fade or darken."

She looked away. "When I was young I remember how bright my father's lines shone. He laughed when I told him. Then they changed. I'm not sure exactly when but I remember how he forbade me to speak about seeing them."

Alric wished she could remember when the change had occurred. Would speaking of the past allow her to remember the day?

He leaned forward. "Maybe Sando can tell us. He chose me for his patrol because he remembered taking my father's classes during his training days."

"Wouldn't he speak to my father?"

"I don't think so. He doesn't always agree with your father's decisions. One of Sando's daughters wants to join the Artisans. Your father said no."

"He said the same to me when I wanted to become a Healer." She put the mug down. "He told me I would become a Defender or I would be sent to live on a farm."

Alric opened his blanket roll. "Why force someone with no desire to fight to become a Defender? When I was chosen to come to the Guild House two girls with no skills or desire were taken for the Defenders. When they were bonded, they broke the bonds and returned to the village."

"There were three girls in my class like that. One was your last bondmate."

Alric removed his sword and knife. He took a honing stone from his pack and checked the edges of his weapons.

"Why was your father banished?" Kalia asked.

"I'm not sure but I think your grandfather wanted to keep him from challenging your father." He tested the edge of his knife. "That was your grandfather's last act as a Swordmaster. There is another matter for us to discuss."

"What?"

"Why do you refuse to duel?"

She refilled her mug. "Do you mean why I refused to face Petan and you stood as my champion?"

He added wood to the fire. Sparks flew to rival the distant stars. "No one would expect you to fight him. I mean your refusal to duel. Is it because you're a woman?"

"Women can become good duelers. Lasara, my younger sister has defeated most of the young men in her class. With a year of experience I'm sure she could defeat Petan."

"So she's good."

"She uses the lines of fire the way you do. She enjoys facing challenges." Kalia met his gaze. "I want to heal not kill. Defenders always take pride in the number of deaths they cause."

Her belief in that statement rang true, but was so different from his experience. "I've never heard any member of Sando's patrol brag about causing a death. They talk about the worthy opponents, the moves of the duel and how lives can be spared."

Kalia unrolled her blanket. "My father fought and killed twenty men in duels and other men who were outlaws when on patrol. He used to demonstrate the kill strokes to show Robec and Petan what to do. I've heard the Swordmaster crow about his prowess."

"And yet Robec has never been part of a patrol or engaged in a duel except the one with me. How will he be able to follow your father without experience?"

"He will have Petan to make the kills."

"Petan has been banished."

"For now." She lay on her blanket.

Alric walked to her side of the fire. "Do you realize the men honored on Ingathering Day didn't kill? The only reason I have a death on my record is because a defeated opponent tried to stab me in the back. My duels have always been without a death. Your ideas are wrong."

She yawned. "Since you don't understand why I

refuse to duel, tell me why you do."

"For justice. To settle disputes. To punish those who wrong others."

"But the men you fight are farmers, shopkeepers or herders. They have no training with sword and knife. They can't win."

Alric laughed. "You have no idea of the reality of the duel. In every village classes are held in the use of weapons. I trained with the other youths and my father taught me. Some of my companions came from the nearby farms for training."

"I didn't know that."

"The people who can't settle their differences with the help of a Judge can name a member of the patrol to stand in their stead. No one without experience takes part in a duel."

Firelight flickered over Kalia's face. Alric clenched his hands. His attraction to her flooded his senses sending desire to tighten his groin. He couldn't gather her into his arms and devour her with his mouth, caress her skin and plunge into her secret places. The bonding bracelet his father had given him burned against his chest. He couldn't use that bracelet when they bonded. That would stoke her fears.

He needed to break the tension. "If you won't duel, how will you use the lines of fire?"

She wrapped her arms around her bent knees. "There is so much more that those of us who can read the lines can do instead of fighting. You touched my cheek where my father hit me. No bruise formed. Somehow you drew blood away from the area. You stopped the blood spurting from Robec's wound."

"I did those things but not all who can see the lines can do the same. We can fight for justice and discover how to perform such acts. Though all Defenders have lines, not all can see them."

"What do you mean?"

"Those who are heart bound can see their mate's lines. They can see their children's but not those of those who aren't blood related."

She curled on the blanket. "You're saying what we can do is unusual."

"And new. Better sleep now. We'll need to travel fast for the next few days. I'll keep watch."

"Wake me if you tire."

"Will do. When we reach the Defender's Hall we'll exchange bracelets and embark on our plan."

Alric walked away from the fire. He checked the bihorns. He had a special bracelet but he wouldn't give that one to Kalia until she declared the bonding permanent. He knew he had to move with caution because of the way their lines of fire moved when they touched.

Sleep crept over him. He rubbed his eyes and walked the perimeter of the camp. When he reached the road, the scent of smoke tickled his nose. The breeze blew toward him. He heard the snorting of a bihorn and crept down the road toward the sound. When he saw the embers of a fire he whistled a series of notes.

"Alric," a deep voice whispered. His friend appeared from the shadows. "So we meet. Have you found her?"

"Wake Rila and follow me. Just came upon her this evening. There's even some kafa brewed. I'll need to add grain to the pot for morning. We're camped in a glade around the bend."

Ganor shook his mate's shoulder. "Wake. We've been invited to join Alric and Kalia at their camp."

Rila stretched and rose. She and Ganor packed their things and followed Alric.

"How is Robec?" Alric asked.

Ganor chuckled. "He's smart. Rila and I watched the arrival of the Swordmaster's men. Robec complained about his leg and demanded they return him to the Infirmary at once."

* * *

Two days of travel from sunrise to sunset brought Kalia close to the Guild House and a meeting with her father. By the third afternoon she saw the walls of the Guild House in the distance. She braced herself to face her father's wrath. She felt sure he would repeat his demands to bond with Alric and then break the bond. Though she had agreed to Alric's plan, she wondered if she could keep from betraying them to her father.

After leading their bihorns to the stable and caring for them, Ganor and Rila escorted Alric and her to the Swordmaster's office. Kalia entered first. Alric stood behind her. His close presence soothed her fears.

The Swordmaster rose. "I see you found my daughter. Kalia, go to the Women's Quarters. When I want to speak to you I'll send a messenger." He walked toward her.

Though she wanted to remain she knew if he touched her she would obey. She feared she would expose the plans Alric had made. She backed to the door. The way her father's lines pulsed told her he might explode. She left the office and started down the hall, running until she had to stop to catch a breath.

Whispering voices rose from one of the seldom used side passages and caused her to freeze. The voices neared and she ducked into the opposite side hall and prayed the couple wouldn't see her.

What was Petan doing here? She stood in the shadows and peered into the corridor. He emerged and he wasn't alone. Ilna clung to his arm.

"Quiet," she whispered. "Someone might come along and see us. You shouldn't be here."

He pulled her into his arms. "Did you enjoy the meeting?"

"You know I did. Isn't he masterful? The way he made me feel I can't explain. When will I see him again?"

"When he needs you."

Kalia frowned. Who were they talking about? As Petan pressed Ilna against the wall, Kalia's eyes widened. His lines of fire glowed dark and illuminated his face. She noticed Ilna's lines. The pale pink color was smudged with gray.

"Enough," Petan said. "You know what he told you to do."

"To pass what he gave me to others."

"Wrong."

Kalia heard a crack followed by a sob. Had Petan hit Ilna? "He told you names. Alric, Robec,

Sando, Ganor. In that order but you only carry enough for two. Choose wisely."

"As if any of them will allow me close enough to kiss them." She laughed. "I will find two. What if I fail?"

"You won't like what happens. Find a way. He doesn't accept failures," Petan said. "Go. When he wants you again, I'll send a message."

"When you leave for good will you take me with you?"

"My leaving here is not for you to question. Go, unless you want to be caught."

Kalia pressed against the wall and breathed as slowly as she could. She listened until she was sure they were gone. What had just happened and who was this mysterious "he" Petan mentioned? Was Ilna off to find the men Petan had named as her targets? Should she warn them? She couldn't return to her father's office to speak to Alric and Ganor. To do so would mean facing her father's fury over her disobedience.

When he sent for her, what could she do? He had his plans and he could make her obey. Not knowing what to do when she reached her chamber, she stilled her thoughts and walked.

When she reached the Women's Quarters, she gathered clothes and walked to the small bathing room. She reveled in the heated water and the floral fragrance of the soap. There hadn't been a chance to bathe during her time on the road other than quick sponge baths, mostly in cold water. Her skin wrinkled from staying in the pool for so long. She quickly rinsed, dried and dressed. The moment she returned to the main room, a messenger waved.

"What do you want?" she asked.

"The Swordmaster wants to see you immediately after the evening meal."

Why not now, she wondered. At the door of the Women's Quarter she paused with her hand on the knob. If she went to his office now how angry would her father be? She could let him think the trainee had garbled the message. Deciding not to wait she opened the door. She needed to learn if her father knew Petan had found a way to enter the Hall. She knew of at least one secret entrance that allowed a person from beyond the walls to sneak into the grounds.

Kalia scurried along the corridor. The door of her father's office was ajar. Was he alone? She crept close enough to peer inside. Robec faced the desk.

"Fool." The Swordmaster spat the word. "Why did you go with Alric? If you had remained here, when he returned with your sister I could have banished him for being alone with her."

"His patrol leader knew he'd gone to search for her. Sando sent people to follow him."

"That patrol leader couldn't have protested if I'd forbidden Alric to leave the Hall. No one defies me and remains a Defender."

"Alric saved my life."

The Swordmaster sputtered. "He did not. The Healers did."

Robec shook his head. "He stopped the bleeding."

"So he would have you think." The Swordmaster leaned across the desk and grasped

Robec's wrist. "Who saved you?"

In a hollow voice Robec responded. "The Healers."

Kalia's hand flew to her mouth. Alric was right. Her father had some way to control people. She turned to ease away from the door.

"Remember this," the Swordmaster shouted. "Kalia will bond with Alric and break the bond on my demand. Just as his father was he will be banished. Petan will return and claim your sister. He will be your Right Hand."

Kalia fled. She raced along the corridor. Alric had been right about her father. Was the control he asserted over Robec the same thing that happened when she and Alric touched? Would being intimate with him give him control over her lines of fire? Would his darken like those she saw on her father and Petan?

She dashed into the Women's Quarters. Were her fears correct? Why had Petan sent Ilna after Alric and Robec? She was so scared she couldn't cry.

"Kalia," her mother called. "Come and have the evening meal with me."

Kalia knew she couldn't eat. Too many problems faced her. She entered the small dining room and selected a salad and a carafe of kafa. Her mother chose a table in a far corner of the room. Kalia filled her cup and sipped.

"So you will bond with Alric. He's almost as good with sword and knife as his father."

"You knew Alric's father?"

Her mother sipped her beverage. "Alron was your father's friend until that boy arrived. Alron wanted the child fostered but your father and grandfather insisted on keeping him here. Your father and Alron quarreled."

"And he was banished for a quarrel."

Her mother stared at her plate. "Robar decided he was heart bound to Alron's mate. Your father wanted to put me aside and send you, Robec and Kalia to be fostered. That was why they dueled."

"And father won."

"The duel ended with their weapons destroyed, both men injured but neither would concede. Your grandfather banished Alron. His older son vanished at the same time. I thought they had joined the rebels."

"When were Alric's sibs sent away? Do you know where they went?" Kalia inhaled the fragrant aroma of the kafa.

The older woman shook her head. "Your father refused to say unless Jenla bonded with him. She refused, gave me the bracelet and died in the bathing pool. She said Alron would be her mate in death as well as life."

"What did she tell the Swordmaster?" Kalia's hands fisted.

"How can you destroy your friend? One day my children will return. My oldest son will take all you value and the rule of your family will end. When you fall into the abyss of death, your lines of fire will burst into flame and consume all you were."

"Why did you give me the bracelet?"

"To protect my children. You must keep it hidden. If your father sees that one during the bonding ceremony he will harm Alric."

Tightness gripped Kalia's shoulders. Did her mother believe Alric wanted to harm them and bonding would keep her sibs safe? The villain was the Swordmaster and his favorite, Petan. "Alric won't harm us. He's not that type of person. He was alone with Robec away from the Hall and with me, too." She dropped her fork on the plate. "What happens when you visit the Swordmaster in his suite?"

"I don't want to talk about my visits." The older woman pushed her chair back. "I can't even do that right. I'm heart bound to him but he's not to me."

Robec appeared in the doorway of the small dining room.

Kalia tensed. What did he want? Was he still under the leader's control? She rose and went to him. "Is there a problem?"

He handed her a box. "Father has cancelled your meeting. He has something else to do. He wants you to use this bracelet when you and Alric bond."

Kalia opened the lid. Her eyes widened when she saw the tainted metal links. Was that blood? She shuddered. "I can't."

Robec glared. "You must. Father said you should remember your promise."

"Tell the Swordmaster I often think of what he said." In that moment she knew he was no longer her father. "Also tell him a tarnished bracelet would be rejected. I can't break a bond that hasn't been made."

"Why would you do that?" her brother said.

"Don't you understand the plans the Swordmaster and Petan have made. They will destroy the Defenders."

"How can you say that? Petan is gone."

Kalia backed away. "I saw him and Ilna in one of the seldom used side corridors. Beware of her."

Robec laughed. "Don't worry. When I see her I head the opposite direction."

"Make sure you tell the Swordmaster what I've said about this thing." She turned and ran to her room.

Chapter 7

Alric strode to the bathing room where the men of Sando's patrol had gathered. His left arm and shoulder ached. All the days of riding and sleeping on the ground hadn't speeded the recovery process. He'd had no choice. Allowing Kalia to flee with no real destination hadn't been a good idea.

As he slid into the steaming pool heat leached the pain away. He released a groan of pleasure.

Sando handed him the soap. "Finally following the Healer's orders?"

"Guess so. Thanks for sending Ganor and Rila."

"Volunteered. So did the rest of us but didn't think the Swordmaster would approve if the entire patrol rode out. Make sure you exercise every day."

"I'll try."

"You've been requested for an assignment and will be sent off soon after the bonding ceremony. The Chief Justicar has heard complaints about a peddler. So have the Artisans. They've agreed to give you today to celebrate your bonding."

"Be glad to be away from the Hall for a time," Alric said. "Too many curious looks and whispers floating around. I'm sure Kalia will welcome the trip." Though she might not like the idea of a duel.

Sando pointed to the bracelet on the chain. "You using that one during the ceremony?"

Alric shook his head. He leaned closer to the older man. "Not yet. We're declaring for a year's trial.

If we make this permanent I will."

"You must," Sando said. "Don't want to lose you. Anything I can do to help?"

Alric shrugged. "Give her time. Challenge her father."

"No challenge for me." Sando slapped Alric's shoulder. "Glad you're not using the special one. I was a boy when I saw them on your father and his mate's arms. Everyone knew the bracelets were special. Bit of envy going the rounds of the Hall. Wonder what happened to your mother's."

"I've no idea." Alric soaped his hands and worked on his hair. He winced. Reaching behind remained a problem.

"Maybe the Swordmaster has it."

"Doesn't matter. All I need is a common bracelet. Since the bonding is forced, I would rather have had time to win her over."

Sando splashed him. "Are you saying she doesn't favor you or you her?"

"Wrong. I want her but Kalia's afraid of bonding. I wanted to have time to win her trust." He scrubbed his hair and swam to the rinse pool. After drying he donned new buckskin trousers, a dark green shirt and vest.

As he left the bathing room and stepped into the courtyard Robec emerged from the bachelor's area. Alric studied the man who had been his rival. Though not a friend, their stay in the Infirmary had begun an acquaintance that could grow into friendship.

"Ready for the bonding ceremony?" Robec asked. "Just a warning. My father has something planned. He gave Kalia a tarnished bracelet for the ceremony. She thinks the metal was soaked in blood."

Why was Robec telling him this? Would Kalia use the tarnished bracelet? Alric turned away. "Maybe he wants to provoke another duel."

"Why?" The other man sounded puzzled.

"Your father wants me gone from the Defenders." He looked away. How would he react if she gave him the tarnished bracelet? To reject might give away their plans for a sham bonding.

"What will you do?"

"Wait and see what happens." He strode toward the stable. "How have you avoided taking a bondmate?"

"The same way I haven't been assigned to a patrol." Robec's lip curled. "Any time I show an interest in any young woman my father sees her bonded to another. He has selected a young woman who has just begun training."

"So young."

"She'll be flattered and biddable, he says." Robec clapped Alric's shoulder. "Be careful. After the ceremony you will be in danger. Kalia warned me about Ilna. She plans some trick."

"She won't come near me. Her lines are odd. You could be the one in danger."

"She wouldn't dare. My father would banish her."

"Does he listen to you?" Alric wished he could tell Robec his suspicions of Petan and his influence over the Swordmaster.

A puzzled frown changed Robec's face. "I hope

he will. Every time I try to speak to him about what I want to do, I forget why I sought him."

Does that mean the Swordmaster controlled his son by way of the lines of fire? Why did the control fail with some people?

"Alric, over here," Ganor called.

"We'll talk again," Robec said. "Take care."

Alric trotted to where his patrol had assembled. Until the gong sounded he endured his friend's teasing. Once the tones filled the air, he marched with the patrol to the salle. As he entered the large room he noticed the leaders of the other Guilds were present in the stands.

Kalia waited at the front of the stands. Her mother and sister stood with her. Robec scurried from the entrance to join them. Alric surveyed the stands and saw Ilna seated in a front row. The smug smile curving her lips troubled him. What did she plan?

The Swordmaster strode past accompanied by his Right and Left Hands. He stood on the raised platform. "We have gathered to witness the bonding of Kalia and Alric. He fought a duel as her champion to win this honor. His opponent loved my daughter and has a heart bond to her. In defeat he acted rashly and because of demands from the patrols was banished."

Alric frowned. Those were not the simple words for the rite of bonding. Kalia left her companions and walked toward him. He strode to meet her. They faced her father.

"As the rite states I have come to bond myself to Kalia for a year's trial."

Kalia faced him. "I accept the offer of a year and for this amount of time bind myself to you."

The Swordmaster raised his hands. "If either of you wishes to break the bond before the trial period ends you must declare your intentions before me and leave the Defenders to find a new home."

Kalia opened the clasp of a gleaming brass bracelet. "And if we choose to make the bond permanent, we will declare this before the Defenders present in the Hall."

The leader of the Defenders glared. The lines of fire shone like bands of ebony. "You will either break or mate this bond permanent in the salle before witnesses. You know what you must do."

"I do." Kalia fastened the bracelet around Alric's arm.

He took a similar one and clasped the brass links on her arm. He held their hands high so all could see. He led her to the patrol. They marched from the salle to the refectory for the nooning.

Once they reached the dining hall the members of Sando's patrol welcomed Kalia with hugs and hand clasps. She smiled. Several called for Alric to kiss her. He leaned forward. Though inches of air separated their lips he felt the sizzle and watched the way their lines sought to mesh. He pulled back.

"You call that a kiss." Ilna reached for Alric. "Let me show you how it's done."

Alric jerked away from her grasping hands. "Find another person. I've no desire for the poison you spew."

Her face blanched.

What had he stumbled on? He studied her pale pink and gray smudged lines. Definitely not normal.

Kalia stepped between them. "The kiss was perfect. What Alric and I have is right for us."

The patrol members moved to exclude the other woman, blocking her second attempt to kiss him. She glared. "You'll be sorry."

Alric and Kalia reached one of the long tables. Platters of food lined the dark wood surface. He looked for the Swordmaster but the man hadn't arrived.

Kalia stood on her toes. Alric tried to see what interested her. Ganor stepped aside. Ilna grasped Robec and kissed him.

"No!" Kalia turned to Alric. "Did you see?"

Alric left the table and moved closer to Robec. Then he saw what Kalia had seen. A small dark spot smudged the other man's lines. "I do. Just don't know what it means. We'll keep an eye on him."

"Petan is responsible," she whispered. "When we're alone I'll tell you what I overheard. You need to warn Sando and Ganor to avoid Ilna."

Sando leaned forward. "We usually do, but why?"

"There's something odd about her lines," Alric said. "If you can see the lines of other people, check Robec's. He may start acting like his father or Petan. I think she tainted his lines."

Kalia shook her head. "He'll be frightened. His nature is nothing like theirs." Her eyes filled with tears. I'm worried for him."

Alric lifted a piece of fried poultry. "If he's infected we can find a solution."

"How?"

"Maybe there's something in the Archives." He

turned his attention to the meal.

When he finished his selections he took Kalia's hand. "If you're finished we can leave for my suite."

Sando rose. "We'll escort you. The evening meal will be brought. In the morning report to me and I'll tell you about the assignment."

As they left the refectory the patrol members surrounded them. Accompanied by teasing and laughter they walked to the hall leading to the quarters. Alric glanced at his bondmate. Her cheeks glowed red. He hoped they would find a way to keep others from learning about the sham bond.

* * *

The door of Alric's room closed and shut out the sounds of merriment. Kalia swallowed against the tightness gripping her throat. Alric wore the bracelet she'd given him, not the one her father had ordered her to clamp on her bondmate's wrist. That one had been as tarnished as her father's lines of fire.

Though she wanted to move from the doorway her feet seemed formed from molten rock and fused to the floor. Bondmates united their bodies. She feared that moment. What would happen? Would his lines darken as he leached the vitality from her? She had seen how pale her mother's were when she returned from visiting the Swordmaster's suite. She had seen her own change when Petan had touched her for a moment. When Alric touched her skin there'd been a different reaction. She didn't want to fail the way her mother had but thoughts of allowing Alric to drain her vitality made her ill. Yet a bondmate had the right to join with the woman who wore his bracelet.

Alric moved past her and sank on one of the chairs.

Her locked knees loosened. She walked across the room and stood at the window staring into the courtyard. There was no escape.

"Kalia, don't be afraid. I won't touch you until you choose. Tonight you'll have the bed. I'll sleep on the floor."

She left the window and stared into the sleeping chamber. The massive bed looked wide enough to sleep four. Five pillows lined the headboard.

She sucked in a breath. "What if my father demands proof?"

Alric laughed. "He won't. He doesn't want to know if our bond is real or not."

She nearly joined his laughter but the tightness in her chest wouldn't allow her to relax. She stepped over the threshold and sat on the edge of the bed. Alric's words about the Swordmaster were true.

She released a held breath. Part of her wanted to move into his arms, to feel his muscular body and taste his mouth. A memory of what had happened to their lines chilled those thoughts.

"I won't toss you out of your bed. There's room for both of us."

"And another one or two." His expression changed. Hope flashed in his green eyes.

Her heart raced. Would he agree?

"Only if you trust me."

"If your plan is to work I must." Did he hear the

tiny notes of doubt she tried to hide?

"We must decide how we will act when we're away from the Hall."

Kalia pushed her new fears aside. She didn't understand her scrambled thoughts of wanting and fearing. Memories of the warmth of his touches brought a desire for more. Awkwardness hovered between them. The bonding bracelet she wore on a chain beneath her shirt felt hot. Usually the metal seemed cool. What did the change mean?

"Why do you fear me?" Alric asked.

"Because of what happens to our lines every time we touch. Because of what happens to my mother when she visits my father."

Slowly the words formed. She spoke of all she'd observed. "Scarlet when she leaves. Pale pink when she returns. Each recovery takes longer. There will be a time when she won't recover."

Alric sat on the floor. "Do you remember much about your grandparents? We need to know how long the darkness has filled your father's lines."

"My father was an only child. My grandmother died giving birth. The Healers cut him from her body. I don't remember much about my grandfather. He died not long after Petan came to live with us."

"What about his lines?"

She shook her head. "I don't remember. Maybe I was too young to see them. I first noticed the darkness when I began training. Have you learned anything?"

He shook his head. "We need to investigate."

She rose. "Then we should search the records. Maybe the answers are to be found in the Archives."

"We can't go now. If you think the teasing was rough earlier, just wait. If we spend our first evening of bonding reading old records you would want to hide and never emerge." He pulled off his boots and stretched out on the far side of the bed.

Kalia stared out the window. What were they going to do? Until she knew what the changes meant she couldn't be with him.

Had she really seen dark spots on Robec's lines? Was he destined to follow his father's path? Every year the Swordmaster became more of a cruel dictator. If Robec had the same changes ahead the Defenders were doomed.

As the sun set and shadows gathered, Alric rose. He lit several lanterns. A knock on the door roused Kalia. "Yes," she called.

"Your evening meal."

She waited a few minutes before opening the door and lifting a heavy tray from the wheeled cart. Alric appeared and took the load from her. She bent and retrieved two covered pitchers. The aroma of kafa made her realize how hungry she was. She's been too tense to break her fast and too nervous to eat much of the nooning.

Alric laughed. "Guess they thought we'd be starved."

Kalia's eyes widened. The tray held a tureen of soup, a platter of meats and cheeses, an assortment of breads and salads. A half dozen fruit turnovers had been squeezed in.

"We'd better do our best." She slipped into the small necessary off the sleeping chamber. When she returned Alric took his turn.

He set several selections of meat and cheese aside. "For later. In case we wake and are hungry."

Kalia added some other selections to his choices. They ate in silence. She waited for her appetite to fade but it didn't. She ate more than she imagined she would.

Alric gathered the dirty dishes. "I'll leave these outside."

She reached for the kafa. "This stays."

"It'll be cold."

"Cold works as well as hot to help me move into the morning. Wonder what tomorrow will bring?"

"Sando mentioned I'd been requested for an assignment for the Artisans and the Justicars."

She leaned forward. Did that mean she'd be here while he went off? "Any idea how long you'll be gone."

"Not a clue and we'll both be going. Bondmates travel together."

She couldn't stop the smile. She would be away from the Swordmaster and his plots. Exhaustion swept over her causing her to yawn. "I'm for bed now."

"I won't be long behind you." He removed his vest and opened his shirt. "Hope you don't mind. Sleeping in a shirt makes me feel like I'm being strangled."

Kalia caught a glimpse of a bracelet dangling from a chain. She wanted a closer look. Did it match the one she wore? If so, what did it mean?

When she returned from the necessary wearing her long nightgown, Alric lay on his stomach. His slow even breathing showed her he slept.

For a time she stared at the long scar across his back and arm. How livid the mark appeared. She nearly ran her fingers along the ridge but recalled what happened with their lines and pulled back. What was she thinking? In sleep, his had stilled. She held her hand above his back and watched the gathering of scarlet. She studied her hands and found her lines gravitated toward his. Were the patterns the same?

More ideas to consider and more worries to fear. How she wished she could creep from this suite and visit the Archives. She'd spent many nights there reading. Could she and Alric spend time there before they had to leave?

She walked to the bed and lay as close to the edge as she could without tumbling to the floor.

* * *

Kalia woke with a start and found herself wrapped in Alric's arms. Tension rolled through her body. His chest pressed against her back. One of his legs rested over hers. Heat spread from his hand resting on her belly. She dare not move or even take a deep breath.

His hand slid away and he rolled to his back. Kalia slid away and hoped she wouldn't wake him. How could she explain the burning of her face or the way her breasts thrust against her nightgown?

The sun had risen. She'd slept all night, a feat unusual for her since the day the Swordmaster had revealed his plan for her to become Petan's bondmate.

She gathered her clothes and scurried to the sitting room and filled a mug with cold kafa. A jolt from the now bitter brew spurred her to move. With the mug and her clothes she entered the necessary to wash and change.

When she returned to the sleeping chamber, Alric sat on the edge of the bed. "Ready to face the day?"

She yawned. "Think so." She lifted one of the fruit turnovers from the plate and took a bite before refilling her mug.

Alric grabbed several pieces of cheese, meat and bread and ate. He poured citren and drank the contents of the glass. "The kafa is cold and the citren is warm." After finishing the sandwich and two of the tarts he gathered his clothes and went into the necessary. When he emerged he carried the remains of the food and set them on the cart. He gestured to Kalia. "Time to go."

As she followed him she thought of how her life had changed.

Chapter 8

As he and Kalia entered the refectory, Alric braced for the teasing remarks of his patrol. He chuckled when Kalia headed to the line and filled two mugs with kafa. If he drank that much of the aromatic beverage he knew he would be as tight as a strung bow.

"More kafa? Wasn't two cups enough?"

"Barely," she said. "I'm not awake until I've had four or five mugs. That's usually how I break my fast."

"That will change now you're part of a patrol." Alric carried his loaded tray and sat beside her on the bench where the rest of the patrol had gathered.

Ganor grinned. "Had a bit of a sleep-in?"

Other remarks flowed around the table. Alric laughed. Kalia's face flushed as scarlet as her lines of fire. Good thing the others had no idea of what hadn't happened behind the closed doors of the suite.

Sando leaned forward. "Meeting as soon as you eat."

"How many?"

"Two Artisans and a Justicar."

Alric turned to Kalia. "You may need more kafa."

"Why are we meeting them?"

"They haven't said." Sando scowled. "The Artisans don't want what happened to spread through the Guild House, so the two of you will need to keep quiet until the problem is solved."

Alric mopped his plate and rose. He and Kalia walked with the patrol leader to one of the small meeting rooms. Lanterns on the wall cast shadows throughout the room. Three men sat at the table in the center of the room. Sando closed the door.

The Justicar studied them. "Do you believe sending them out so soon after the bonding is right?"

"It's best," Sando said.

"Truth."

Alric drew a deep breath. He'd forgotten the Justicars' talent of being able to tell if what a person said was with true or not. "Is this a sealed complaint?" he asked.

"Yes," one of the Artisans said.

Sando turned to the Artisan. "Alric and Kalia will lead the group. He is the dueler. Explain the problem."

The older of the Artisans leaned forward. "There is a peddler who has been warned twice about selling shoddy goods and claiming they come from our stores. He has also sold experimental inventions."

The younger Artisan raked his hands through his brown hair. "Some of the inventions have proved dangerous."

"There have been reports about this trader cheating on weights," the Justicar said.

Kalia gasped. "I traveled for a few days with such a peddler but I left because I didn't like his practice of that of his drivers. I believe I witnessed a theft."

"Truth. Name."

"Hosar."

The brown-haired Artisan pushed his chair back. "Why would the Defenders send an escort for such a man? I see no reason to look to them for help."

"The Defenders didn't send me. I well, let's say I needed to be away from the Hall for a time." Kalia pressed her hands on the table. "If we face him, I can swear to some of the things he did."

"Truth," the Justicar said.

Alric leaned toward the Artisans. "Just what do you want from us besides bringing him back for punishment?"

The older Artisan stared at the table. "We must learn who from our Hall is dealing with him and providing the peddler with goods to sell."

"How do you wish this handled?" Sando asked.

"By a duel." The older Artisan slapped the table. "Hosar refused to heed repeated warnings."

"I accept and will do my best," Alric said.

Kalia looked at the table. "I should be the one to face the challenge."

Alric brushed her hand with his fingertips. She stiffened and he drew back. How long would she fear this bonding? "Since you're new to a patrol and have never dueled for justice this isn't a good time to learn." He looked at the three men. "We can be ready to leave by midday. How many will join the party so I can arrange supplies?"

The Justicar walked to the door. "A Senior and Junior Judge and two trainees from the Hall of Justice will comprise our party." He paused. "I'm passing a warning for caution to you. Rumors have reached us of a banished Defender who travels as one of the peddler's drivers. You may want to send more than one pair."

Kalia frowned. "I thought those who were released were sent to one of the distant villages."

Sando chuckled. "Not all those stay where they are sent. Some join the various rebel groups. Others become outlaws and prey on travelers and isolated farms."

Alric turned to the Artisans. "How many in your group?"

"Since we don't know who can be trusted, both of us will go." The older pointed to his companion. "He will check the goods and I will investigate the inventions. We must discover our traitor."

"Do you think he'll tell us?" Alric asked.

The Artisan smiled. "This is the way of justice and we have confidence in your reputation as a dueler."

Alric nodded. He'd seen the outcome of many duels and watched the questionings by the Judges. "With the size of the party I'll arrange for five pack beasts. Do those who travel with us have steeds or should the Defenders provide them."

The Justicar turned. "We have our own."

"So do we and ours are easier to control," the older Artisan said. "Since the carts left from our gate we'll meet you there in three hours. Carry your nooning to eat on the way."

Alric watched the men from the other Guilds leave. He turned to Kalia. "You'll have to pack enough clothes to last a week. With luck we'll find a village where our clothes can be washed during our travel. Sorry we won't have time to transfer your things to my suite."

Kalia stepped back. "Are you sure I shouldn't stay in the Women's Quarters while you're on this assignment?"

Sando coughed. "I'll start organizing your supplies. You can explain the ways of our patrol to her."

Alric rested his hands on the table. "The women and men who are members of Sando's patrol and aren't bonded stay in their own suites in our section of the first wing. When they choose a mate they decide which suite to use. Since you have none, we will live in mine. Except for special assignments the unbonded remain in the Hall. All bonded pairs travel together."

"Even if there are children?" she asked.

"We try to keep the patrol staffed with enough pairs so those with small children remain in the Hall and are on leave until the children are old enough to enter training. If the parents must take an assignment, there is always someone staying behind. The children stay with these members. During our last tour we had three pairs on leave."

"Is your patrol the only one that does this?"

"Don't know. I've been part of Sando's patrol since I left the training school."

"Other than clothes is there anything else we'll need?"

"Maps of the roads the peddler used but Sando will have the supply master provide them. You should bring anything you need for amusement. The Artisans we'll travel with this time are tinkers rather than performers. Traveling with that segment of the Artisans can be lively."

"Will there be a Healer with us?"

"They only leave their Hall when they have reports their service is needed. We have an aid kit and there are herb men and women in the villages who have some skill and were trained at the Healer's Hall." He winked. "You and I will be there to stop excessive bleeding."

"Should we? Our ability is looked on as evil."

Alric stepped back. "Who told you that?"

"The Swordmaster forbade Robec, Lasara and me to talk about using our lines for any reason. He said I would be banished if the other Defenders knew what I could do."

"My patrol knows about me and is pleased. I've saved several of them." Was this one of the reasons the Swordmaster wanted to banish him? Alric wondered why the leader of the Defenders would scorn something that could help the patrols. Could the Swordmaster read the lines?

Kalia walked to the door. "I'll go for my pack and arrange to have my things packed and join you. Where?"

"The stable." He watched her walk away. During their days of travel he intended to find ways to gain her trust. She had slept most of the night in his arms and feeling her body curled into his had felt right. Their lines of fire had flowed in harmony. He was heart bound to her and he suspected that the reverse was true. Until she was willing to speak of the bonding aloud, he would wait.

He exited the meeting room and strode to the supply depot. Sando stood in the doorway. He turned to

Alric. "You're set. Basic supplies ordered."

Alric nodded. "Did you include hunting and fishing supplies? If I remember the farms in that area are poor."

"Snares and fish traps included. Also dart throwers."

"Good. Make sure there's plenty of ground kafa. Kalia drinks several mugs to wake." Alric paused. "And maps." He entered the supply depot and pointed to the one on the wall indicating the area he wanted. The map showed marks for farms and villages.

The agent pulled a tube from the shelf. "Here you are. If you find new places, mark them."

Sando walked beside Alric. "Pack beasts are on the way. They'll be loaded by the time you pack. Where's your mate?"

"Gone to the Women's Quarters for her pack and to arrange for her belongings to be delivered to my suite. Can you check them in?"

"No trouble."

Alric strode to his suite and examined his pack. He dashed to the patrol bathing room for shirts, two vests and pair of trousers. Having time to wait he went to the refectory kitchen for two noonings. He selected a flask of kafa for Kalia and one of citren for himself. As he strode to the stable he thought of ways to gain her trust.

* * *

Kalia left the meeting room and dashed along the twisting corridors to reach the Women's Quarters.

A sense of freedom filled her. For several weeks she would be away from the Swordmaster and his threats. Could she learn more about the lines of fire and the reaction she'd noticed between hers and Alric's while they traveled together?

Waking in his arms had made her feel safe. The moment had lasted a brief time and brought a yearning to join with him. Could she act on these new and exciting moments before she understood what was occurring with their lines?

She opened the door into the lounge and stopped short. Lasara ran to meet her. "Why are you here?"

"To fetch clothes for an assignment and to arrange for my things to be packed and moved to Alric's suite."

"You mean you're not staying here."

"Not the way of his patrol."

"Do they have their own Women's Quarter?"

"Bonded pairs live together and those who are waiting to find their mates have their own chambers."

"Wow. How nice. I'll pack your other things and call for someone to take them to his place."

"Thanks. Why aren't you in class?"

Lasara scowled. "Father decided to test the young men. I'm as skilled as any of them. He said there was no need to test me since my bonding will take place soon."

"What?"

Lasara nodded. "That's what he said. He'll won't tell me more, he's not taking chances this time."

Kalia drew a deep breath. Surely their father couldn't mean to bond his younger daughter to Petan.

But Petan was gone and banished. "Did he say who?"

"No." Lasara walked away. "I know this much. If I don't like who he chooses I'll run and I won't be caught like you were."

"I'll help you." Kalia caught up. "When I return I'll visit and we can make plans."

"Good. All I want to do is join a patrol and duel."

Kalia patted her sister's arm. Though she didn't understand Lasara's love of the duel she would support her desire to become a functioning member of a patrol.

As they walked down the hall to Kalia's sleeping chamber, Ilna emerged from hers. She halted with her hands on her hips. Kalia noticed a silvery sheen to Ilna's pale pink lines.

"Thief." Ilna spat. "You took the mate promised to me. You won't have him for long." She laughed. "He can't even stand to kiss you. You'll be sorry when I'm the Swordmaster's mate."

"Why would my father want to choose you?" Kalia asked.

"Who wants an old man past his prime? He won't be Swordmaster forever and Robec doesn't have the nerve to fight for his right. You'll learn who will rule here. Won't be long before there's a change." She stepped closer, grabbed Kalia and kissed her. "Pass my gift to your bondmate."

For a moment Kalia was too stunned to move. She wiped her hand across her mouth. "I'll do no such thing." She pushed past and dashed into her chamber. Ilna's laughter followed.

Lasara scowled. "That was ugly. Why did she

kiss you?"

"I don't know." Kalia sank on the bed. "Oh, no." Was that a dark spot on her lines like the one she'd seen on Robec's? Anger and fear spouted like water from a broken pipe. The darkness spread. Slowly she calmed her escalating emotions and the spot stopped enlarging.

She filled her pack with Lasara's help. To the clothes she added a record book she'd taken from the Archives in hopes of learning more about the lines. Maybe there was something about the infection Ilna had passed to her.

"Is there anything you don't want taken to Alric's suite?" Lasara asked.

"Leave all the bedding except the quilt here. The rest of my clothes and things from the closet go. Pack all my soap, lotions, jewelry and knickknacks. She lifted the box containing the tarnished bracelet. "Don't take this."

Lasara peered inside. "Where did you get this?"

"Father. He wanted me to give it to Alric."

"How odd. It's ugly. I'll toss it in the trash heap."

Kalia laughed. "A fitting place. While I'm gone, be careful. Don't fight with Father. Where's Mother?"

"Visiting him."

Kalia shuddered. "So soon after her last time." Though she feared for her mother, nothing would change the older woman's devotion to her bondmate. She hugged her sister. "As soon as we return I'll visit you. Take care of Mother."

"I will."

Kalia hoisted her pack and hurried to the stable. Alric led two bihorns outside. Mist had been saddled.

"Am I late?"

"No. We're meeting the others at the Artisan's gave." He stowed her pack and blanket roll behind the saddle before giving her a leg up. He handed her a cloth wrapped packet and a flask. "Nooning and kafa."

"Thank you."

A stableman led a string of loaded pack animals to where they waited. Alric tied the lead rope to Storm Cloud's saddle and led the string into the tunnel. Kalia followed the train.

By the time they reached the Artisan's gate the rest of the party had arrived. Alric transferred the lead to one of the Artisans' steed. He led the group onto the road with Kalia at the rear of the procession.

As they rode, she wondered what the assignment would bring. Could she and Alric find a way to break the uneasy truce? She liked him. With the sting of a biting bug a thought struck. More than liked but she had to blunt all her emotions, especially now. Still, her thoughts centered on her bondmate.

Alric was the only man she could join her life to forever. So many problems loomed. Her father's threats against her family, Petan's continued existence, Ilna's passing of the infection. How much more trouble would buzz into her life?

When they reached the side trail she caught up with Alric. "Along this road we'll pass two farms where the peddler stopped and three where he didn't. There is a small village where I left them."

Alric motioned to the Justicar. He relayed what

Lines of Fire

Kalia had told him. "She can show us which farms."

"Our complaint came from a village," the Senior Judge said. "We'll listen to the farmers and see if there are other unjust actions. The more we have, the more justified a duel will be."

At the first farm Kalia was surprised when one of the farm workers tried to make a false claim.

"Sold me a belt that broke the third time I used it," the man said.

"False," the Junior Judge said.

The man opened his mouth and only garbled sounds emerged.

Kalia turned to one of the Justicar trainees. "How did he do that?"

"Guild secret," the girl said.

Before long they left the farm and made camp in a clearing beside the road. Kalia watched how Alric organized the camp, assigning each member to a different task. She went with him to set snares.

"Won't our catch spoil during the day?" she asked.

"We'll cook what we find before we leave and the meat will be our nooning."

"That's a good idea. The peddlers traveled slowly and every day stew was cooked for the nooning."

"Then we should catch them before too long."

As he straightened she admired the way he moved. Her thoughts filled with what ifs. She had a year to find answers and perhaps one of those what ifs would come true.

* * *

At the end of a week of travel with stops to collect complaints, they drew closer to the peddler. Kalia noticed more black spots on her lines of fire. Should she tell Alric she had been infected? What would happen if she gave in to her desire to be in his arms? Would she infect him? She decided to isolate herself more completely from the others.

"We should catch up with the peddler within a day or two." Alric sat beside her. "According to the map there's a large village about that distance away."

They had been on the road for seven days. "Then you'll duel," Kalia said.

He nodded. "It's the way. What troubles you? You've grown so quiet."

She stared at the ground. "I'm worried about my mother. She was with the Swordmaster when I left. I told you how faded her lines are when she returns. She insists she can't do what she should in the right way because he's not heart bound to her."

He reached for her and she evaded him. "Does she love your father?"

"Yes and he believes he's heart bound to a dead woman." She closed her eyes. "There are things I should have told you but there hasn't been a right time." She leaned back and told him of Ilna's meeting with Petan and his orders. "He knows how to enter the Hall through a secret entrance. I followed him once years ago."

"When we return show this entrance to me and I'll tell Sando."

"There's more." Would he recoil with horror? "When I went for my clothes Ilna attacked me. Look at my lines."

His expression made her want to cry.

Chapter 9

Alric couldn't stop his reaction. A chill rolled along his skin. His mouth gaped. The flowing lines on Kalia's skin showed several dark spots, the same shade of dried blood as on her father's and Petan's lines.

"Are you sure Petan is behind this?"

"Who else? He named you, Robec, Sando and Ganor. She failed with everyone but Robec and now me. What am I going to do?"

Her voice became a shrill whisper. Alric watched the darkness spread. What he saw was perhaps deadly. He felt helpless. There had to be a cure. "Let me think about what to do. For now, we need to solve the matter of the peddler."

"I could stay here until you finish this assignment."

"I can't let you do that. Is there anything that triggers the darkness to spread?"

"Emotions."

"Then try to remain calm."

She nodded. "I'll try. I don't want to become like them." Tears flowed over her cheeks.

Though Alric was tempted to take her into his arms he feared her reaction would cause a rapid spread of the spots. He went to the fire and filled a mug with kafa. He sweetened her cup with honey and added a small amount of salopa. If she slept unless she had a nightmare, the spread of the taint should halt.

* * *

At dawn the members of the party stirred. Before long they'd eaten the morning meal, loaded the pack beasts and prepared to leave.

Alric helped Kalia into the saddle and took his place at the head of the group. "I'll ride ahead to see how far the village is. The map isn't very accurate." Being alone might give him an idea to chew over about this new development.

Petan and the Swordmaster's lines held no glint of scarlet. Kalia's sported only a few dark spots. How many days, months or years would be needed for the process to be complete?

Since Petan was much younger than the leader of the Defenders, Alric tried to remember when he'd first noticed the change in Petan's lines. He couldn't recall a time when his enemy's lines had been scarlet rather than darker.

That meant nothing. He hadn't known Petan since childhood and even during the training days there'd been little contact. Petan had been two classes ahead. Alric forced his thoughts away from the other man.

What could he do? He was heart bound to Kalia. The moment their gazes had meshed he had known. They had a year before she must make a choice. The thought she might walk away caused a lump to cluster in his gut. If she broke the bond he would flee and join the desert riders.

Heart bound. Why did those words bring a flash of hope for Kalia? Her mother was tied by love but the

Swordmaster wasn't. Alric searched the information Kalia had told him about the lines. When the older woman returned from her visits to her bondmate her lines were drained of vitality. Did he take something from her he needed to survive?

A frown tightened his brow. Petan had the same lines. How did he feed his needs? Alric wondered if Kalia knew.

What would happen of both people were heart bound? Had Kalia made a choice she feared voicing? Her father's threats against her family might force her obedience. Alric wondered if he could persuade her to admit her love for him.

Not yet. She didn't trust him. When they were alone they could talk. He would observe her lines. If he must he would give her essence from his lines. He halted the bihorn and waited for the others. "The large village is just ahead on this road. If we're lucky we'll find the peddler."

"Are you sure?" one of the Artisans asked.

"Yes."

"Then we ride," the Senior Judge said.

As a unit they galloped down the road. When they reached the first house shouts spurred Alric ahead of the others. He reached the village commons and encountered a milling mob.

"What's happening?" he asked.

Several men stood beside saddled bihorns. "Thieves," one yelled.

"Justicars are on the way," Alric said.

Moments later the rest of the party arrived. Men and women shouted.

"Silence," the Senior Judge shouted.

"The peddlers cheated," a woman cried. "Took my honey and traded for spices with a false bottom in the boxes."

"Jewelry went missing from my shop," a man said.

"When did they leave?" the Judge asked.

"Camped outside town last night. Finished trading at sundown. Was late when they left the tavern." The older man took a deep breath. "I'm one of the village elders."

Alric gestured to Kalia. "Come, we must force them to return."

The Junior Judge nodded. "I'll ride with you."

Alric turned his bihorn toward the road. When he spotted three wagons in the distance he prodded Storm Cloud into a gallop. He reached the first wagon and turned his steed to halt the wagon.

"By order of the Justicar you are to return to the village for judgment."

"Why should we?" a sharp-face driver asked.

"If you fail to obey, the Defender will kill your animals," the Junior Judge said.

Kalia rode to Alric's side. "Will you?"

"If forced but don't worry. I doubt they will try to force me to act."

The driver of the rear-most wagon complied with the order as did the second one. The sharp-face man scowled. "Move and I will turn. Cart beasts are too slow to get away. We have done nothing wrong."

"False," the Junior Judge said.

Alric edged Storm Cloud to the side of the road.

Kalia rode to the Junior Judge's side and led the caravan back to the village.

By the time they reached the commons many of the villagers had gathered on the grass of the benches surrounding the dueling circle. The Senior Judge gestured to Alric. "Food is available in the tavern. Once you've eaten we'll start the investigation."

Alric nodded. He followed Kalia and the Junior Judge into the log building. He waved away a large nooning platter of meat, cheese, bread and a variety of salads.

"Soup and citren will be enough," he said.

Kalia frowned. "Why aren't you eating more? We broke our fast at sunrise."

"A hearty meal makes a fighter sluggish."

"What about your recent injuries. Will they impede you?"

The concern in her voice heartened him. He began to believe there was hope the bonding would last.

"Depends on my opponent. Could be you. If so I'll quickly disarm you."

Her eyes widened. "You would fight me?"

"Happens when there's no one else."

"Then I'm in luck. One of the drivers is a former Defender. I thought I recognized him when I traveled with the peddler. Before Robec and Petan entered training classes he taught them."

"Then he's sure to have some skill with sword and knife. Didn't he teach you?"

"The Swordmaster's daughter received no special training. Lasara's abilities have confounded him." She leaned closer. "Can you win?"

"I believe so." He felt positive but bragging often led to mistakes. "Good thing Petan didn't cut my sword arm."

"Just be careful."

"Always." Again, the concern in her voice encouraged him to hope. He finished the soup and drank the citren. Then he waited for his companions to complete their meal. They left the tavern and joined the Senior Judge.

The man rose from a bench. "The investigation of the charges against Peddler Hosar will begin. May truth and justice prevail. First I will hear the complaints."

One of the trainees read the list of verified complaints gathered during the journey. Then he called on the villagers and heard from them. "Truth," he said to each complaint.

One of the Artisans rose. "This is the third time Peddler Hosar has been accused of the same crimes. We know he's working with one or more members of our Guild. The Artisans want the name or names of these traitors."

The Senior Judge nodded. "Peddler, what do you say about the charges? Are you willing to provide the information?"

"Yes."

"False," the Junior Judge said.

The Senior Judge approached. "Give me the name of your Artisan supplier."

"Can't give a name."

"Truth."

"Can't or won't?" the Artisan asked.

The peddler shrugged. "Never saw him. Leaves notes for me with instructions to burn them."

The Junior Judge nodded. "Truth."

"Describe the notes," the older Artisan said.

"Say where the goods will be left."

"How do you pay?"

"Leave coins beneath a rock. Other goods like honey, salt, gems and metals are put in a box."

Each of his statements was accompanied by "truth" from the Judges.

The Senior Judge faced the peddler. "Twice you have been warned about selling shoddy goods and using false weights. You know the penalty for a third offense."

The older Artisan turned to the Judge. "Since our information hasn't been provided I call for a duel."

"Agreed." His companion joined him. "If he loses he will help by setting a trap for the traitor."

"If I win, I will go free."

"That is in accordance to the rules of Investia," the Senior Judge said.

The peddler grinned. "Worth a try. Valdon, present yourself."

The tall, lean, broad-shouldered man stepped forward. He wore a sword and knife. He moved with the ease of a trained Defender. Though he was older than Alric, he remained in his prime. Alric had no memory of seeing the man since his arrival at the Hall. Kalia's quick intake of breath brought a realization. This was the man who had trained Petan and Robec.

A sly smile crossed Valdon's face. "I'll fight her."

"You don't have the choice." The Senior Judge turned to the Artisans. "Your champion."

"Alric."

Alric removed his shirt, vest and chain. He folded them and left them with the trainees. He faced his opponent.

Valdon kept his shirt on. He unsheathed his weapons.

Kalia moved to Alric's side. "He won't fight fair. Years ago, he cut Robec and the wound festered. Be careful."

"I will."

Valdon laughed. "So the Swordmaster's daughter remembers me. Is this man your bondmate? I thought Petan wanted you. How happy my favorite student will be when he learns I killed the man who took what was his. I'll be a Defender again as a reward."

"Petan fought me and lost," Alric said.

"He struck from behind like a coward and was banished," Kalia added.

Valdon laughed. "Perhaps when I finish this duel and win I'll find him and we can form a band. Be better than driving a peddler's wagon."

"Why seek Petan?" Alric asked. "Join one of the rebel groups."

"They're fools. Strong leaders are needed. Petan is that. There are more of my kind than you realize. The bonding rules send many a good man away in disgrace." He strode to the circle in the center of the commons.

Alric followed. "It's time."

"Luck," Kalia called.

Alric joined his opponent in the circle where every year the youths of the area were tested. The Senior Judge stepped between them.

"The fight will continue until one of you is disarmed. No death duel. Fight for justice." The older man stepped from the circle.

Alric raised his sword and met Valdon's first stroke.

* * *

Kalia hoped Alric had taken her warning seriously. She moved to the edge of the circle where Alric faced Valdon. The clang of metal on metal reached her.

Valdon's sword moved like a striking snake. Kalia nearly missed seeing his knife cut a slash along Alric's chest. Her hand flew to her mouth. Shouts from the peddler and his companions mixed with groans from the other spectators. Kalia tensed. She turned and saw Hosar's smirk.

The cut energized Alric. His sword flashed so fast the blade blurred. The singing sound, the flashing movements held Kalia spellbound. Before long Valdon's shirt hung in tatters. Small cuts dotted his chest and arms.

After the initial wound Alric received no more. Kalia focused on the lines of fire on the men's skin. She saw the smooth flow of Alric's. Valdon's patterns moved erratically. Alric sent Valdon's blade flying from the circle. He caught the knife with the tip of his sword and it fell to the ground.

"Yield," Alric shouted.

"Yielded." Valdon held both hands in the air.

The Artisans bound his hands and those of Hosar. The peddler scowled. The Justicar trainees led the men from the commons.

The Senior and Junior Judges spoke to the drivers of the wagons. Each man or woman was awarded one of the cart beasts and a few coins as their wages. They were allowed to gather their belongings. The Artisans began an inventory of the contents of the wagons. All articles of value were stored in sacks.

Though fascinated by the process Kalia left the commons to find Alric. He sat at a table in the tavern. He reached for his shirt. She shook her head. "I need to check your wound."

"Only a shallow cut. Bleeding stopped early during the bout."

"Didn't you listen when I told you about Robec's wound? I'm speaking as your bondmate. I want to clean the cut."

Alric grinned. "Get the aid kit."

When she returned he sat with his back pressed against the edge of the table. She opened the kit and poured alk on a piece of linen. She ran the swatch over the wound and felt pleased when no bleeding began. She saw no redness of swelling around the area but the injury was too fresh to show any signs of a problem.

"Happy?" Alric asked.

"For now." She wished she'd been able to clean the area before the lesion closed. "Keep an eye on the area for several days." She touched the end of the wound with a finger and saw the lines coalesce in the area.

As she moved away she felt pulses of desire surge through her body. She closed the aid kit and hurried to return the small pack to the supplies. If the Swordmaster could see how Alric's presence changed her lines the threats would become real. She couldn't allow that to happen.

Kalia strapped the pack in place. She glanced toward the prisoners. The peddler sat with his head pressed against his bent knees.

Valdon beckoned. "Will you treat my wounds?"

"Why should I?"

"Your bondmate stopped the bleeding. Come closer and see if dressings are needed. I would welcome the touch of your soft hands."

She stiffened. Though his hands were bound she feared he might attempt an escape. "If the bleeding has stopped there is no problem. I'll send the herb woman to you." She walked away.

He laughed. "Surprised me to learn your father permitted a bonding with another man. Petan was always his favorite and the man chosen for you."

"Petan was never my choice. He dishonored his sword and knife to attack from behind. He wounded my brother and tried to plunge a sword into Alric's back. He's been banished."

"Are you sure he's gone. Petan is a natural leader. He draws men to his side. Women, too."

Kalia strode toward the tavern. What did Valdon mean? Did he know about Petan's manner of gaining entrance to the Hall? She'd seen and heard him lurking in a seldom used corridor. Had his banishment been a sham arranged by the Swordmaster to quiet the demands of the patrol leaders?

By the time she reached the commons, the Judges and Artisans had finished their tally of the peddler's goods. Two of the cart beasts were loaded with goods to be taken along to repay those Hosar had cheated. Two more would bear the prisoners.

Kalia approached one of the trainees. "What will happen to the peddler and the defeated champion?"

"Hosar will be sent to the Isle. The other one may be shipped there, too. The four Guild leaders will pass sentence on those who break the rules thrice. Valdon has been twice caught aiding someone who breaks the laws of Investia."

Kalia frowned. The Isle? She'd never heard of such a place.

Alric waved. "There's food waiting in the tavern. After we eat we'll return to the grove where we camped last night."

She joined him and watched the amount of food he ate. She shook her head. "Do you have room for all that?"

"Don't worry. Some of the dishes aren't served in the Hall. The dulceberries don't travel well." He lifted one of the thumb nail size purple berries to her mouth. "Taste one."

She took it between her lips. When she broke the skin the sweet honey flavor tinged with a spice she didn't know produced a sigh of pleasure. She took a second. "They're wonderful. I wonder if they would grow in the greenery."

"Never thought of that." He ate another. "When I was younger I used to sneak into the patch when they ripened and eat until I couldn't move. So did my friends."

Kalia sighed. Spending her entire life in Defenders Hall except for an occasional outing to ride Mist or field trips in training had isolated her from such adventures. "I wish I could have had friends and special times."

"You'll have them now."

She stared at her hands. For a year if that long. The Swordmaster's threats would steal any chance of escape.

She finished eating and helped Alric bind the prisoners in the saddle. She let him herd the pair to the camp while she led the pack animals.

* * *

In the morning as Kalia saddled Mist she glanced at her arms and gasped. The dark blotches had spread. How long before the lines reached the dark dried blood color of the Swordmaster's? Would Alric see the taint and walk away or would he try to give her his essence the way her mother fed her bondmate's lines of fire? Would Alric break their bond and escape to the rebels?

Chapter 10

The journey back to the Guild House took longer than the search for the peddler had taken. Each time they stopped at a farm or the small village, some new claim was made. Alric groaned. The Judges had the trainees question each claimant again. Practice, the Senior Judge had said and a way for him to evaluate the trainees.

At two farms the Artisans had caused the delay. Once they repaired a pump so it drew water from the ground. The second stop had found them adapting an antiquated plow into a more modern one.

Alric studied the prisoners. The peddler's slumped shoulders and staring eyes shouted defeat. Valdon's alertness bothered Alric. The banished Defender watched every member of the party as though sizing his chances for an escape. Every mile closer to their destination seemed to increase the man's watchfulness. Did he expect a rescue? Was he waiting for some band of outlaws to attack? Alric prodded Storm Cloud closer to the two prisoners.

"So Defender Alric, eager for our return?" Valdon asked.

"Yes."

Valdon laughed. "Hard on a newly bonded pair to be sent on an assignment. The Swordmaster is a clever man. Heard how the patrol leaders forced your match with Kalia. Do you really think she will keep the bond? Once she heeds her father, you'll be out."

Alric ignored the remarks and rode to relieve the Junior Judge who rode point.

"Have you had her yet? Danced on her body?" Valdon's voice rose. "I think not and I believe you will never succeed in seducing her. She was promised to Petan. Why would she want you?"

Though Alric felt tempted to slam his fist into Valdon's mouth he continued his steady ride toward the head of the group. He refused to engage in a battle of words with a banished man. Still, he wondered why Kalia had avoided him since the day she'd cleaned his wound.

As if on cue, the area on his chest where Valdon's knife had cut began to burn and itch.

That evening soon after they made camp Alric carried the fish traps to the stream and lowered them into the water. With luck there would be fish in the morning to be cooked for the nooning.

He tore off his vest and shirt. Scooping handfuls of cold water he splashed the liquid over the injury. The momentary relief brought a sigh. His eyes widened. Lines of fire avoided the area. What did it mean? He donned his shirt and slung the vest over his shoulder. The cracking of leaves and twigs caused him to turn around.

Kalia stood with her back to him. She appeared poised for flight. "Is something wrong?" he asked.

She turned. Tears cascaded over her cheeks. "Look at my lines." She rubbed her hands over her arms. "Soon they'll be as dark as the Swordmaster's."

Alric stepped closer. "There must be a way to stop the spread. Can your mother's visits to your father halt the spread of his?"

She gazed into his eyes. "Would you have me drain you and keep you from using the lines when you duel?"

He clasped his hands behind his back to keep from reaching for her. "What would happen if the heart bond is mutual?"

Her voice caught on the edge of a sob. "Then my mother, sister and brother are doomed."

"Not unless we exchange bracelets again and vow to last forever. That must be done publicly."

She edged away. "He would know. He will make me tell. No matter what I do someone will die." She bolted back to the camp.

Alric leaned against the rough bark of a towering spruce. There must be a way to help her. There were a few days of the journey remaining for him to devise a plan. Once they reached Defender's Hall he must speak to Sando. Could he convince his patrol leader to challenge the Swordmaster?

When he reached the camp he sat with the others and ate stew. His appetite fled. Five forced bites were enough. Before retiring he checked the prisoners and returned to the fire for first watch. His head throbbed. Stings like sparks from the fire prickled along the edges of the healed knife wound. When the moon rose above the trees he woke the Junior Judge and a trainee and went to his blanket.

* * *

Angry clouds rolled across the sky. Dark

blotches surrounded the sun. Alric put the fish he'd caught in the traps and cooked on pieces of flat bread for the nooning. They would have to eat as they rode which meant freeing the prisoners' hands.

"Finish quickly." He stiffed the food in several leather pouches. "We'll need to move fast if we want to find shelter before the storm hits. There is a farm five or six hours ahead where we can shelter tonight." He passed the food to the others and kept the prisoner's provisions on his bihorn.

Long before they reached the farm, the downpour began. Alric urged his companions to push their steeds to the limit. Thunder rolled across the sky but the flashes of lightning flared in the distance. Water saturated his vest and shirt. Finally, they clattered across the farmyard and headed to the barn. The Senior Judge, Kalia and the female trainee halted at the house and dashed to the door. Alric herded their mounts along with the pack beasts to the barn.

He slid from his steed, checked the prisoners and allowed them to change into dry clothes before re-binding their hands. After tending to the steeds and unloading the pack beasts he found time to change. The area around the wound was swollen and some of the tissue had turned dark. Once he reached the Hall he needed to seek the Healers.

He climbed to the loft to arrange sleeping space. The others who had taken shelter in the barn joined him.

The Senior Judge and two young men arrived carrying kettles of thick soup and kafa. Alric took travel bread, cheese and honey from the pack. The Judge sat beside Alric. "The women will spend the night in the house."

Alric nodded. He turned to the farmer's sons. "Thank you for the hot meal." He handed them a copper coin. "Tell your parents this can be redeemed at the Hall."

After seeing the prisoners fed Alric forced himself to eat. He drank two mugs of kafa hoping the beverage would keep him awake until his watch ended.

When he finally reached his blankets he hovered between heat and chills. Nightmares of his enemies and fights he'd won and lost woke him all too often.

* * *

As they set out the next day he noticed Valdon's smile. Did the failed Defender know what his single cut had done? With grim determination Alric remained in the saddle. Finally the walls of the Guild House appeared.

They entered the Justicar's gate. Alric remained mounted when the others dismounted. The prisoners walked with the Judges and the trainees. Alric turned his bihorn into the tunnel to Artisans Hall. There all but the supply beasts followed the two men.

He and Kalia continued through the tunnel. As they passed Healers Hall he considered stopping but he needed to care for Storm Cloud. When they emerged from the tunnel they rode to the stable.

Kalia dismounted. "Are you coming? After we tend to our steeds, don't you have to take your record book to the Swordmaster? Then we'll have enough time to reach the refectory for the evening meal."

"I'm coming." Alric slid his leg over the saddle. His feet hit the ground and the rest of him followed.

* * *

Kalia turned. Her eyes widened. "Alric." She knelt beside him. His only response was a moan. She didn't need to touch his skin to feel the radiating heat. His lines of fire had paled. Those on her hands pulled toward him.

"No." She wouldn't drain his vitality. "Help! Someone help."

One of the stablemen dashed into the open. "Who did this?"

"He wasn't hurt. He has a fever. Can you take care of the steeds?"

A trainee ran across the yard. Kalia waved to him. "Run to the Healers. Tell them there's a man down. Burning with fever. Just returned from an assignment. Dueled. Small slash. May be infected."

The young man ran into the tunnel.

Kalia rose and paced around Alric's body. Time dragged. She peered toward the tunnel opening. The urge to touch him warred with the fear that doing so would harm him. A pair of young men in Healer blue emerged. Relief nearly brought her to her knees.

Once Alric was on the litter she followed the men to Healers Hall. A Senior Medico waited. "Did he open the wound on his back?"

Kalia drew a deep breath. "Two weeks ago he fought a duel and received a shallow knife cut. His opponent is the same one who injured Robec a dozen or more years ago. My brother had the same reaction to the slash. This is my fault. I should have insisted on cleaning the area even though the blood flow had stopped and clotting had occurred."

A pair of trainees removed Alric's vest and shirt. When Kalia saw the dark edges around the wound and the angry swelling her hand flew to her mouth.

The Medico shook his head. "And you didn't suspect how ill he was."

"He didn't complain."

"Defenders." The dark-haired man snapped orders. "He's dangerously ill." He sent the trainees for instruments and medicines. He washed his hands with soap and water, then soaked them in a basin of alk.

The pungent aroma of the clear liquid made Kalia cough. Her eyes widened when the Medico took a knife from the basin and opened the skin along the slash.

Yellow-green exudates oozed from the wound. The trainees used pieces of alk soaked cloth to clean the area.

Two trainees held Alric's arms and two held his legs. The Medico poured a stream of alk on the wound. Alric bellowed and bucked with his body nearly falling from the table. In an instant the seizure stopped. The healer spread a blue ointment on a piece of cloth and placed it on the open wound.

After the shout and near convulsion Alric remained completely still. A chill rolled over Kalia's skin. What would she do if he didn't recover? The idea made her rub her arms to warm herself. The Senior

Medico stepped back to allow the trainees to dress the wound. "Take him to a private room. A cooking bath now and every three hours until the fever is lowered." He turned to Kalia. "The next three days are vital to his recovery. You will be permitted to remain in his room."

Kalia looked up. "I will stay but I must take the report book to the Swordmaster and speak to Alric's patrol master."

"Do that and be sure to return. Your presence will help."

Kalia nodded. "I'll return as soon as I can."

With haste she trotted through the tunnel and into the stable. She paused to feed Mist and Storm Cloud a few apelons before carrying two packs to Alric's suite. She found her belongings had arrived. Though she wanted a long and leisurely soak in the baths, she washed in the necessary and changed. With Alric's report book in hand she left the room.

As she stepped into the courtyard a trainee shouted. "Defender Kalia, you are to report to the Swordmaster."

"I'm on my way." Her shoulders slumped. She had wanted to see Sando first but she had no choice. She strode to the main door and knocked.

"Enter."

Kalia stepped inside and closed the door behind her. "Our report book. Sorry for the delay. I saw my bondmate to the Infirmary." She set the book on his desk. "The assignment was successful and informative."

He laughed. "Was more than that. I hear your bondmate is ill. The Healers expect him to die. What a clever one you are. Death is better than banishment. It's said you should never leave an enemy at your back."

Kalia fought to control her reaction to his glee. He wanted Alric to die. "I wasn't told he was dying."

"He will and you will be free. I will return to my original plan."

She grasped the edge of the desk. "Your original plan?"

"Of course. With Alric dead you'll have no mate. I'll make sure of Petan's return and you will bond with him."

A chill ran over her skin. She swallowed the protests she wanted to scream. His lines of fire were the color of a liver removed from a slaughtered animal. She looked at her own and saw the darkness had spread.

Her father slid his hand across the table and grasped hers. "You will obey me."

She shook her head. "No."

Anger flared in his eyes. "Who did this to you?"

"Did what?"

"Changed your lines of fire into those of power."

She wanted to know more. "And you can see the change. Do you read the lines?"

"No." He grasped her hand. "I can feel your increased power. Who did this to you?"

Kalia met his gaze. "The same person who infected Robec. She was sent by Petan to destroy your son and Alric. Since she couldn't have my bondmate she took me."

"Does Petan know?"

"How could he? I haven't seen him since the

day he disappeared. And I don't ever want to see him again. Maybe Ilna knows where he is." She drew a deep breath. "Just what does this change do?"

"Makes the recipient powerful. Petan will be angry when he learns about you." He released her hands.

Kalia backed to the door. "Did you ever think his plans aren't the same as yours?"

"He and I are in accord. The culprit will be punished. Dismissed."

Kalia exited and hurried away. Before returning to the Infirmary she needed to see her mother. She sped along the corridors and entered the Women's Quarters. To her surprise, Lasara stood outside their mother's chamber.

"Why aren't you in class? Has something happened to Mother?"

"She's recovering from her stay with him."

Her sister's presence made no sense to Kalia. "Then why are you here?"

Lasara scowled. "He removed me from classes. He's angry because during a practice duel I beat Robec. The Swordmaster said I'm too fond of fighting and that was not womanly. I'm to remain here until he finds a mate for me."

"I'm sorry."

"Why? You did nothing. I've a plan and I'll use it. He won't control my life."

"Be careful who you talk to."

"You're the only one I've told." A frown wrinkled Lasara's forehead. "Why aren't you with your bondmate?"

"Alric was wounded and is in the Infirmary. I had to take our report book to the Swordmaster." Kalia opened the chamber door. "I have to ask Mother something."

The older woman sat in a chair beside the bed. "Kalia, how was your first assignment?"

"Interesting."

"Why did you come?"

"To see you before going to the Infirmary to stay with Alric. He's ill from an infected wound."

The older woman clasped Kalia's hands. "Unite with him completely and all will be well."

Could she? Should she? Her mother knew nothing about the tainted lines Kalia bore. "I'm not sure you're right."

"Forget your fears and examine your heart." The older woman looked up. Tears filled her eyes. "I love your father and have from my first sight of him. He wanted to bond with another but she was heart bound to your father's best friend. Jealousy and envy controlled his actions. His father believed your father's tale of this woman being stolen from him. Together they destroyed Alron and tore a family apart."

Was her mother speaking of Alric's parents? "I'm sorry that happened. Was that before his lines turned dark?"

"Soon after. Things were hectic at that time. Petan had just been brought to the hall. Your grandfather was ready to step down as Swordmaster." The older woman frowned. "You must not speak of this to anyone."

"Why not?"

"More trouble will follow."

As if there wasn't enough now, Kalia thought. She kissed her mother's cheek. How could she hold back what she'd just learned from Alric? "I'll return when I can." She hurried away and entered the courtyard.

Sando waved. "I've just seen Alric."

"Is he worse?"

"His fever remains high. They're bathing him in cool water. He opened his eyes but didn't speak. What happened?"

Kalia told him about Valdon and the injury he'd given Robec years before. "Have the Justicars decided what will happen to him?"

Sando bowed his head. "I've heard he'll be sent to the Isle. Go to Alric. If you can help him, try. He's the best of my patrol. If we lose him, more than one man will be lost."

"Before I go, can you help my sister?" Kalia explained what had happened. "I fear she will run, be caught and punished. I think the Swordmaster intends to bond her to Petan."

"I'll talk to several of my trusted patrol members and let you know how we can help."

"Thank you." Kalia dashed through the tunnel. Her boots clicked against the flagstones. As she exited, she stopped to catch her breath. Inside Healers Hall, a young woman directed her to Alric's room.

A trainee rose from a chair at the bedside. "If you need someone, pull this cord and one of us will appear. If his fever rises or his body shakes, call. Those aren't good signs."

Lines of Fire
Page 154

"I will."

Kalia reached the bed. Could she do what must be done? Would her kiss cure or destroy him?"

"Kalia," he whispered.

She leaned toward him. His deep green eyes showed signs of fever and also of his feelings for her. She touched her lips to his.

Searing heat flowed through her. Alric grasped her shoulders so she couldn't move away. Her hands pressed against the dressing on his chest. The kiss continued until she felt faint.

She pulled free and sank on the chair. She studied his lines. They had brightened. What about hers? She was afraid to look.

Alric reached for her hand. "What just happened?"

"Your lines are brighter."

"Look at yours."

She stared at her own. Much of the darkness had vanished. A smile formed. There was a cure. She must tell Robec to search for a dual heart bonded mate.

Alric released a held breath. "I don't know what you did but I feel much better. Will you stay here tonight?"

"Yes."

Chapter 11

The kiss told Alric everything he wanted to know. The heart bond between them was true. He studied the lines of fire on her skin and saw how much of the darkness had vanished. "Do you see what our kiss did?"

Her eyes filled with tears. "He will know and will carry out his threats."

Alric captured her hand. "Will he attack Robec before he has another heir? First he needs to break the bond with your mother."

"I'm not sure he can. He could have done that years ago. Why would he wait?"

Alric closed his eyes. "Maybe he can't. He has a need for what she gives him when she visits. I wonder how he views Robec's infection. As a bonus or something else?"

"I tried to tell him Petan planned for Robec's lines to be tainted. I don't think he believed me."

"The taint may protect your brother from being controlled by your father and Petan. Did your father notice the change in your lines?"

"He tried to control me and was angry. He doesn't see the lines. He said he could feel the power. He intends to punish Ilna. Why all the questions?"

"Since you're infected Petan can't siphon vitality from your lines. You're safe."

Kalia scowled. "Lasara isn't." She drew a deep breath. "The Swordmaster has pulled her from classes.

He's finding a bondmate for her and I think I know who. She plans to run away. I told Sando and asked for his help."

"Tell her to go south to the desert riders and ask for Jens. The sooner she goes, the safer she'll be."

"And my mother?"

"She's heart bound to your father."

"What does that mean?"

"Can she leave him? I know my father was heart bound to my mother. Though he remained alive after her death, he always seemed sad. If I hadn't been there, he would have died when she did. I don't think your mother can leave him."

"I fear you're right."

"Speak to Robec about his lines and tell him what he must do if the infection is to be cured." He reached to pull her into his arms.

Kalia pulled back. "Though I want to be close to you this isn't the right time. We can't let my father know the blight can be cured. If he touches me he'll know."

Though what she said disappointed him, the kiss had lessened the amount of dark smudges on her lines. When she'd placed her hand on the dressing over his wound he had felt the swelling lessen. Another treatment by the Medico would complete the healing.

As though thinking about a treatment, the older man entered the room. He carried a glass of wiggling creatures. He turned to Kalia. "Excuse us. I have a treatment prepared."

She walked to the door. "How long will this take?"

"An hour should be enough."

"Go talk to Sando," Alric said. "Tell him about our earlier conversation about where a person should go."

"I will."

Alric closed his eyes. He'd seen the eaters of dead flesh used once before. The way they'd removed the damaged tissue without touching the healthy area had amazed him. His closed eyes kept him from watching the wiggling pale creatures being placed on his chest. Light touches on the area made him shudder. Alric clenched his fists.

He must have dozed for when he opened his eyes no wriggling creatures festooned his chest. "Done?" he asked.

The Senior Medico nodded. "You'll have another scar that will fill in and fade over time. One question. During the fight did you find using your left arm difficult?"

"Was a bit slow but I haven't practiced much. You should check my opponent's knife. Not sure how he managed to infect me. Was such a shallow wound."

The man nodded. "Already done. His knife had a hollow tube filled with foul matter. The Artisans are studying the mechanism. It's like nothing they've ever seen."

Alric grimaced. "We don't need something like that added to our weapons."

"Agreed but they think there would be other applications." The Medico paused at the door. "If you remain fever free for another day you'll be released."

Alric liked that idea. He rose and walked around

the room, down the hall and back. Using the back of the chair for balance he began a series of squats.

Laughter sounded from the doorway. "Do you ever stop?"

Alric turned. 'What brings you?"

The patrol leader stepped inside and closed the door. "There's been a bit of trouble."

"Swordmaster?"

Sando slumped on the chair. "Not this time. Valdon is gone. He wasn't in his cell this morning."

Alric retreated to the bed. "Petan?"

"Who knows?" A frown furrowed the older man's brow. "Why him? He was banished weeks ago."

Alric explained the connection between the two men. "Kalia has seen Petan in the halls at least once since he left. She said he knows a secret way to enter the Hall."

"Matters may be coming to a point where a challenge must be made."

"When?"

"No one feels angry enough yet."

Alric rested his hands on his thighs. "Kalia and I need another assignment. We need to be away from the Swordmaster's sight for a time."

"Why?"

"He has threatened to break his bond and choose another mate. Lasara, Kalia's younger sister wants to run. We fear she'll be the next daughter the Swordmaster offers Petan. Kalia will tell her about the desert riders and Jens."

Sando nodded. "Kalia spoke to me about her sister and I have a plan to help the young woman escape."

"Good. I'll tell her."

"Tell me what." The door closed with a click.

Sando rose. "Tell your sister to come to the courtyard after moonrise. Our patrol has the gate. Ganor will escort her to the pasture. A travel pack, a map of the southern quadrant and a steady bihorn will be waiting."

"Tonight? She's frightened because the Swordmaster will name her bondmate tomorrow."

Sando nodded. "Have her meet Rila outside the baths for the Women's Quarters. She'll escort her through the corridors." He grinned. "Some of us know a few of the unused passages."

Kalia nodded. "I'll go to her now."

Once she left, Alric nodded to the patrol leader. "Any ideas for an assignment. Being away from here when the Swordmaster learns his younger daughter has vanished is a good idea."

Sando nodded. "There's one I'm considering. The Justicars came to me rather than the Swordmaster. Eastern quadrant. Farmers losing produce and livestock during raids. Travelers stopped and robbed. Women raped. The worse things happen five or six days travel from here. Want me to send out someone to investigate and discover where the outlaws are hiding."

"Should we try to capture the leaders?"

"How?"

"Send pairs out to surround the area and pick a central spot for them to meet."

Sando frowned. "Don't think that's wise yet. Just you and Kalia go."

"What about the Swordmaster?"

"Won't tell him until we have something to report." He patted Alric's shoulder. "How soon will you be free?"

"Possibly tomorrow."

"I'll check back then."

Alric watched Sando walk away. Had Valdon found some way to join these outlaws? Did they have someone inside Defenders Hall providing them with information?

* * *

Kalia hurried to the Women's Quarters via a seldom used corridor she had discovered years ago. She stepped inside and spotted Lasara. With a nod Kalia followed her sister down the hall to the empty room that had been hers.

"What's happening?" Lasara asked.

"Escape plan for you." Kalia quickly outlined the things Sando and Alric had told her. Kalia crouched and began to draw in the dusty floor. "These are the halls you and Rila should use to reach the courtyard. Once you leave ride south. Seek the desert riders and ask for Jens. Tell him Alric sent you. Alric believes he's his brother fostered to a shepherd by our father."

Lasara's deep green eyes filled with tears. "Thank you. Thank Alric. I'll miss you. Will I ever see you again?"

"Just believe you will."

"Does Alric really think this Jens is his brother?"

Kalia nodded. "He felt a connection between them when they dueled. If you can learn if Alric's suspicions are true he would thank you."

Lasara reached beneath her tunic. "Let me show you the bracelets I found when I cleared your closet. A piece of the flooring came loose. I found these stuffed in the small cranny."

Kalia studied the copper bracelets. "I remember reading something in the Archives about copper bracelets but I can't remember what or where."

"I wish I knew who hid them there. They must have belonged to some Defender bondmates."

"Keep them. When you find the bondmate of your dreams, use them instead of the ordinary brass ones."

"I will."

Kalia hugged her sister. "As you travel, be careful. Hide by day and ride at night. Stay alert."

"I promise and I'll find a way to send a message to you. Maybe I can discover if this Jens is Alric's sib. I like your bondmate."

"So do I. If you can learn about the relationship you'll help him redeem a promise he made to his father." Kalia went to the door. "I'd better return and hear what the Senior Medico says about Alric's condition."

As Kalia scurried along the corridor to reach the forecourt, the gong assembling all the Defenders present in the Hall clanged. What should she do? Should she accept the call and go to the salle or hurry across the courtyard and run to Healers Hall? While she paused to decide, the door of the Swordmaster's office opened.

The leader of the Defenders stepped into the corridor. "Good. You're coming with me."

She stared. "I'll stand with my patrol."

His laughter sounded like the braying of a cart beast, the stolid animals used to pull wagons. "Won't be yours much longer. Though your bondmate lingers on this side of the abyss he will soon die."

Kalia stared at the floor. He didn't know that Alric grew stronger every hour. She wanted to gloat but kept the information inside. "Until that day I'll stand with Sando's patrol."

"Doesn't matter where you stand. Be prepared to face a duel. Ilna stands accused. Her fate is in your hands."

"Of what is she accused?"

"Betrayal. Seduction. Attack with malice. Failure to obey orders." He dug his fingers into Kalia's arm and marched her to the entrance to the salle. "Go stand with your patrol until you are named. Though your lines darken and protect you from my control in this you will obey."

Kalia broke away and ran to where Sando's patrol stood. What could she do?

"Why aren't you with Alric?" Sando asked.

"I went to give Lasara the instructions and stayed longer than was wise. The Swordmaster dragged me here." She rubbed her arms.

"Any idea why he summoned us to assemble?"

"He plans to force a duel."

"Who will be the contestants?"

Kalia felt acid rise in her throat. "Ilna. Me. I

don't want to duel."

Sando scowled. "Why does he want you to fight?"

She rattled off the charges she had been told. Though she wanted to tell him about her lines, she refrained. "Are they really grounds for a duel?"

"All and defeat means banishment. Did she really attack you and your brother?"

"Yes. Why does the Swordmaster name this as my duel? Robec can be the dueler."

Sando groaned. "He can't challenge her until three months have passed since he stood as her champion. I doubt any man will accept her call for a champion."

Rocks tumbled in Kalia's gut. How could she fight a duel when she hated the thought of facing another with sword and knife? Would the duel increase the darkness of her lines? She and Alric's encounter had partially banished the taint but some remained and would grow because of her fear and anger. She stared at the lines.

The Swordmaster followed by his seconds strode into the salle. Kalia stared into the stands. Students, women and those not assigned to a patrol sat on the benches. None of the other Guilds were represented. Why?

The Swordmaster raised his hands. "Ilna, present yourself."

The young woman sashayed from the stands. "Do I get to choose my mate today?"

"Not today or ever. You stand charged of the following offenses." He recited the list.

She laughed. "What was wrong with kissing Robec? He stood as my champion. As for Kalia, the kiss was to congratulate her for deftly stealing the man I was promised. Did she complain?"

"Others witnessed the attack. Should I call them to testify?"

Ilna raised a fisted hand. "You don't understand what happened. People only tell you what you want to hear. The man who will be Swordmaster commands my loyalty."

Robec leaned on the railing separating the stands from the floor. "I ordered no such thing. Since you chose me as your champion, I can't challenge you no matter how I wish for the chance." He vaulted to the floor. "Kalia, unfortunately you must face her."

Sando clasped her shoulders. "You must or Alric will be ordered to leave the Infirmary. He and Robec will be forced to duel again."

Kalia rubbed her hands. Though she hated the thought she had no idea of Alric's present condition. Though he healed, he hadn't been discharged. For him to defeat her brother would infuriate the Swordmaster.

"I will face Ilna in the circle." She forced her voice to emerge emotionless and clear.

The other woman's laughter resounded from the salle walls. "When you lose, all you possess will be mine."

The three other patrols left the arena floor and sat in the stands. Kalia drew deep breaths. What if she failed?

Sando bent his head closer to her ear, "Be careful. She may have a blade like the one Valdon used.

Several times she's been missing from the Hall for days."

Kalia nodded. "Other than during practice, I've never dueled."

"You know the forms. Remember Alric's trick if you have any skill reading the lines. Haven't seen her fight but I've a feeling she's erratic and not skilled. I know she refused her father's offer to teach her."

Kalia unsheathed her sword and knife. She walked to the circle where the other woman waited with the Swordmaster and his seconds.

"The Left Hand will judge."

Kalia stepped over the barrier to enter the circle. She faced Ilna. I can do this, she repeated silently until she felt confidence infuse her thoughts.

"Let the bout begin."

Ilna charged forward. Kalia knocked her opponent's sword aside and evaded a knife thrust. At first her moves were defensive. Then the rhythm of the sword dance took over. Practiced but seldom used moves became natural. She watched Ilna's lines of fire and began to sense what her opponent planned. Kalia struck her opponent's knife and knocked it from the young woman's hand. Next Kalia sent Ilna's sword flying from the circle. Ilna dashed to retrieve the weapon and stepped over the barrier.

"Out," the Left Hand shouted. Duel ended. Kalia wins."

"Not fair," Ilna screeched.

"You left the circle."

"To get my sword. Can't fight without one."

The Left Hand confiscated the blade. "You

know the rules. You've dueled before. You are the loser and are banished. A bihorn and a pack with enough supplies for five days awaits you at the gate."

"Where will I go?"

"The choice is yours."

Ilna stooped and picked up her knife. The blade flew toward Kalia who fell to the sand and rolled across the ground.

Sando helped her up. "You all right?"

"She missed."

The Right and Left Hand grasped Ilna's arms and led her away. Kalia brushed sand from her clothes and walked with Sando's patrol from the salle. Behind her she heard congratulations from the members of the patrol and a few shouts from the stands.

Once they reached the courtyard, Kalia thanked Sando. She jogged to the tunnel and ran to Healers Hall. At the door to Alric's room, she eased the wooden barrier open. He sat on a chair beside the bed. "Everything set for your sister?" he asked.

She nodded, "She knows what to do." For a moment she hesitated. "I fought a duel."

"You what?"

She sat on the floor beside the chair and told him about her afternoon and the meeting with Ilna in the salle. She held out her hands. "The dark areas on my lines have grown."

"I can see. Why?"

"My anger for being tricked into the duel and the feelings the fight with Ilna raised."

He leaned toward her. "We can unite."

She shook her head. "Not yet. As soon as we are

off on our next assignment."

"Why not now?"

She stared at her hands. "The Swordmaster will know. He forced me into the duel with Ilna. I think he knows what emotions do to the blight."

Alric nodded. "I fear you're right."

She knew she was. Something puzzled her. She thought of her childhood. Had Petan been the one to infect the leader of the Defender? She hadn't liked or trusted him from the first meeting.

Chapter 12

Alric stretched and turned on his side to stare at Kalia. In sleep, she looked at peace, except for the dark smudges on her lines of fire. He hated to wake her but noises from beyond the door predicted they soon would be roused by Healer trainees. He brushed her hair from her face. Her eyes opened and she gasped.

"Are you all right? Do you need a Healer?"

"I'm fine. The place is waking. They'll be here soon with a morning meal and to check my condition. You have time to duck into the necessary."

She slid from the bed and scooted to the small room. When she returned her hair had been braided. She sat on a chair beside the bed.

He missed her warmth. Though she had slept in her clothes he'd felt her breath on his skin and the warmth of her body. His sleep had been sporadic. Being awakened by erotic dreams and being unable to act on his fantasies had taken will power. He couldn't wait to be away from Defenders Hall and in a place where they could be alone. He felt his erection grow. He groaned and walked to the necessary.

He had just returned to the bed when the door opened. One of the trainees carried a wooden tray and set it on a small table that fit over Alric's hips. "After you break your fast the Senior Medico will arrive and check your progress." He paused at the door. "There's enough for both of you."

Alric grinned and motioned to Kalia. "You can

have the kafa. Citren's mine."

"Are you sure?"

"I know how you are in the morning. Groggy and grumpy."

She laughed. "That's me." She filled a mug, inhaled and sipped. "Wonderful."

"When we head out this time I'll tell the supplier to pack double kafa."

She snagged a piece of toasted bread and spooned plum preserves over the slice.

Alric drizzled honey on the cooked grain and covered the serving with cream. He studied Kalia's lines. Fewer dark splotches this morning than when she'd returned from the duel. If they encountered the Swordmaster would he notice?

When they finished the meal, Kalia carried the tray into the hall. The Senior Medico arrived and examined the wound. "You are fit to leave." He handed Alric a jar of salve. "Wash the area and apply this daily. Will keep the tissue supple."

When the man left Alric grinned. "My clothes. Sando brought clean ones."

Kalia took them from a drawer. She retreated into the hall and waited for him to join her. They left Healer Hall and hurried through the tunnel.

When they emerged an uproar greeted them. One of the four patrols currently in residence stood beside saddled bihorns. The Swordmaster faced them. "You will find her," he bellowed.

Alric turned to Kalia. "What's going on?"

"Looks like Lasara missed her morning meeting with him. She must have vanished from the Woman's

Quarters. I hope she's all right."

"Will he accuse you of helping her?"

She shrugged. "Who knows what he'll do. Seeing another of his plans go awry suits me." She pointed to her arm. "Because of this blight he can't force me to talk."

"Just be careful."

The Swordmaster strode toward them. He grasped Kalia's arm. "Where is she?"

"Who?"

"Lasara. She has vanished."

"She has?"

Alric turned his head to hide a smile. Kalia's widened eyes and gasped words were the perfect response.

"She was to meet me this morning to learn about her bondmate and she failed to arrive. She's not in her chamber and her mother knows nothing about where the girl went. Lasara's sword and knife are gone. No one has seen her. Where did she go?"

"How would I know?" Kalia spoke in a soft whisper. "I've been at Healers Hall with my bondmate."

The Swordmaster scowled. "Your mother informed me you spoke to your sister yesterday."

"I saw her in the Women's Quarters. She was angry because you pulled her from the training classes. She likes to duel." Kalia gasped. "She said she would run away. I never thought she would."

The leader of the Defenders whirled. He stomped to his seconds. "Send the assembled men to search. Divide them into four groups to check the main roads of the four quadrants for news of the runaway. Tell them she must be found."

Was that fear he heard in the older man's voice? Alric touched Kalia's hand. With a nod of his head he indicated they should go. Once they were away from the crowd he halted. "We must find Sando and learn where our assignment will take us. Otherwise I fear your father will demand we join the search for Lasara."

"What if his patrol has also been assigned to the search?" she asked.

"We'll leave with them and separate. Finding the source of the trouble in the eastern quadrant is vital."

Moments later they arrived at the provisoner's storehouse and found Sando waiting. "Things set?" Alric asked.

Sando chuckled. "No problem arranging supplies with the stir over the girl."

"Will she be safe?" Kalia asked.

"Two of our best are trailing her. They'll leave false clues for several days and then return."

"Thank you."

"You two head to your quarters and pack. I'll arrange supplies and maps."

"Extra kafa," Alric said. "Seems my bondmate doesn't move in the morning without several mugs."

Sando laughed. "I'm the same. I'll have your steeds saddled."

Kalia halted. "Mist doesn't like others messing with her."

"I'll manage. Have a way with bihorns." Sando waved them away. "Attach yourself to one of the search parties."

Once they reached the suite, Alric unloaded the packs while Kalia found fresh clothing. A knock on the door startled him. Alric turned to answer. Kalia stopped him.

"What if the Swordmaster has sent for me?" she asked.

"We'll face him together." He opened the door.

Robec stepped inside. "Imagine you've heard about Lasara."

Alric nodded.

"I wanted to join the teams searching for her," Robec said. "My leg is completely healed and strong. Father refused to let me leave the Hall. Why did Lasara run? She was the best trainee in her class."

"Father ended her training because he found a bondmate for her. Since Ilna corrupted my lines I'm no longer of use to the Swordmaster so he'll give Lasara to Petan."

Robec rubbed his hands together. "She did this to you?" His eyes narrowed. "You are infected."

Alric grabbed Robec's arm. "There is a solution."

"What?"

"Find your heart bound and bind her to you," Kalia said.

"Here?" Robec's shoulders slumped. "Father will see me bonded to a woman of his choice."

"A chance will come," Alric said. "I don't know when or how but you won't be lost to darkness. You must remain calm and keep anger and other negative emotions at bay. That will show the progress of the change."

"How do you know?"

"I've seen Kalia's grow when she's angry or afraid and remain stable when she's calm." Alric hoisted his pack. "Why did you come?"

"To warn you to be careful. Petan visits Father. They have a plan to destroy Alric."

"I know Petan visits," Kalia said.

"I know both men want me gone from the Defenders," Alric said.

"Kalia, he still wants you."

Alric lifted Kalia's pack. "I won't let him have her."

Robec opened the door. "Good luck with whatever you're going to do."

Alric heard yearning tinged with envy in Robec's voice. Why was the Swordmaster stunting his son's development? Was the leader really the villain?

Kalia released a sigh. "I wish we could help him."

"He needs to leave the Hall to find what he seeks."

She nodded. "As long as that man remains in control Robec will remain trapped here." She took her pack from him and stepped into the corridor.

When they reached the stable Sando waited with their saddled mounts and a pack beast. "There's a group leaving to search for Lasara. Join them." He handed Alric a map. "Here's your route with several alternate roads marked if you need them."

Alric helped Kalia into the saddle. He led the three animals to the gate, mounted and joined the departing group. At the first crossroads he turned his bihorn onto a trail heading east. He felt a sense of relief to be away from the Hall and away from questions from the Swordmaster.

They rode through the day with a stop to eat a midday meal and allow their steeds to graze.

"We're free," Kalia said.

"For now."

"Will we camp out or find an inn?"

"We'll camp tonight at a nice place. You'll see." He winked.

As the sun moved westward Alric pointed to a barn off the road. "We'll spend the night here. The barn's a regular stop for Defenders." He rode Storm Cloud up the lane toward the structure.

Kalia followed. Together they unloaded the pack animal, groomed and watered the animals and left them in stalls. After starting a fire in the pit Alric carried their packs and blankets into the barn.

He climbed the ladder to the loft. After tossing several forkfuls of hay for the steeds he broke open a bale and prepared a nest for the night. He spread one of the blanket rolls over the hay and left the other at the end of the bed. On a hood fastened to a post he found a lantern. After checking the well he climbed down and distributed the hay to the animals.

Preparation done he returned to the fire and helped Kalia with the meal. While gathering greens he found a bush with sweet-smelling roses. Using his knife he cut several sprays of the scarlet flowers.

When he handed them to Kalia her face turned as red as the blossoms. He sat beside her. "Are you afraid of me?"

She shook her head. "Never of you but of what the Swordmaster will do when he sees my darkness is gone. He will know."

"There's nothing he can do to you." He filled their bowls with stew and tasted his. "Better than when I cook."

She filled two mugs with kafa. "Sorry there's no citren. Would you rather have water?"

"This is fine. Tastes like you."

She laughed. "And how is that?"

"Smooth with a bit of sweetness and a little spice. Intriguing. And much better than when I'm the brewer. They never let me cook when the patrol is on rounds."

Once they finished the meal and cleaned the dishes, Alric banked the fire. Kalia set a pan of mixed grains and water on the heated stones.

"To break our fast in the morning."

Alric rose and took her hand. "Come with me." He noticed her hesitation and tugged her closer. "There's no rush. We'll go slow." He drew a breath. "I'm heart bound to you."

She gasped. "You are?"

Did she realize the reverse was true as well?

She cleared her throat. "I'm sure where my heart lies. I have fears about what we're about to do. What if I infect you with this blight?"

"Then we'll seek a cure together." He led her to the ladder and climbed behind her.

When they reached the top and moved away from the edge he turned her to face him. He ran his fingers over her face. "If you wish there's a lantern I could light."

"I'd rather not."

Alric drew her into his arms and stared into her eyes. He felt tremors of fear. He brushed his lips over hers. No matter how much he wanted to rush and possess her he would go slowly. With his hands he stroked her back and caressed her lips with his tongue. She opened to his explorations. The sweet and spicy flavor of kafa and the scent of some floral combination nearly made him move too fast. He felt his erection swell.

Slowly he released her. He slid her vest from her shoulders. After removing his, he pulled his shirt over his head.

Kalia touched the shallow indentation from the knife wound. She bent her head and kissed along the scar.

Alric pulled her into a tight embrace. He felt the tips of her breasts brush his chest.

A gentle kiss took fire. He drew her closer. Her body moved against his, Alric drew a deep breath filled with the essence that was hers alone. The fire in his loins grew hotter until he could think of nothing but Kalia.

He stepped away to remove his boots and trousers. His rod sprang free. In Kalia's gaze he saw hesitancy and eagerness. He met her gaze. "All I have is yours."

She slid her divided skirt over her hips and saw to remove her boots and skirt. He knelt at her side. One of her fingers touched his erect member. Alric fought the urge to push her down and thrust inside.

He stroked her breasts with one hand and ran the other over her belly. Her gasps became sounds that dared him to tangle his fingers in her nether hair.

"Then all I have is yours," she whispered.

He claimed her mouth in a kiss that made her tremble. Fear of eagerness, he wondered.

* * *

The kiss sent surges of heat to every corner of her body. Kalia followed his lead. Her tongue slid over his. She strained to touch her skin to every inch of his. He raised his head to catch a breath.

Tremors of fear made her quiver. She opened her eyes and stared at her lines of fire. The kisses and caresses had erased much of the dark stains. Joyous laughter turned to fear. Had Alric's lines darkened? She started to speak but his lips claimed hers. Heat rolled from his mouth and from his hands that touched, stroked and caressed. His fingers reached the curls guarding her secret place. One hand moved along her thigh. He touched a place and sent a steady current of fire through her body.

Her breath came in short gasps. She wanted more but didn't know how to ask. His hands slid beneath her hips.

"Almost there," he whispered.

The words vibrated like the wind whispering through the leaves of a tree.

He raised her hips. His thick erection slid over her folds. One thrust, then two. The third made her gasp.

His mouth covered hers. His tongue thrust and retreated in a rhythm that captured her. She bent her knees and pressed her feet against the blanket and entered the rhythm of the dance. Waves of heat became a conflagration.

As the fiery blaze consumed her, Alric raised his head. A shout, part agony and part ecstasy erupted. Her cries echoed his. He collapsed, rolled to his side and held her close.

For an instant or a long time they pressed body to body while the fires banked and their gasps became slow and even. Kalia stared at their lines of fire. The scarlet threads moved in harmony. All the dark smudges had disappeared from hers and none appeared on his. The copper links on the bracelets they wore on chains glowed as though the metal had captured the fire.

What did this mean? Sleep obliterated the question.

* * *

The aroma of kafa woke Kalia. She rolled on her side and reached for the mug. After inhaling the savory steam, she sipped. Her gaze moved to assess her lines. Still clear and any signs of lurking darkness were gone. She finished the beverage and washed in the basin of water on the floor beside the make-shift bed. She stretched and felt new aches reminding her of the night, the mutual pleasure and Alric. She dressed, rolled their blankets and emptied the basin. With the mug, blanket rolls and basin, she descended the ladder.

Alric looked up. "Are you all right?"

Her lips curved into a smile. "Perfect. We are truly bonded."

He took the mug and kissed her lightly. "I fear we won't be able to hide our bond from anyone who can read the lines." He re-filled her mug.

She blew across the steaming liquid. "We know that but my lines are clean. Did you know they move in harmony with yours?"

"I noticed that." He dished the cooked grain into bowls and drizzled honey over the top.

"Do you think we'll find these outlaws?"

"Yes." He tasted the sweetened porridge.

She swallowed a bite. "What makes them different from the rebel bands?"

"Rebels have drawn apart because they don't like the rules. Though they are known to raid and steal they would rather trade. They don't separate into Guilds the way we do but live together. Outlaws prey on people taking what isn't theirs and often kill for fun."

As soon as they finished eating they packed and left.

* * *

For three days they traveled past farms and camped in groves where there were fire pits. On the fourth day they entered a large village.

Alric pointed to an inn. "We'll spend the night here."

They stabled and cared for their bihorns. When

the stableman approached to help Mist barred her teeth.

"Step back," Kalia said. "She's skittish."

Alric leaned closer. "A one rider steed?"

She nodded. "Won't tolerate another rider. At least she let Sando saddle her."

"He's a genius with bihorns. Never seen one he couldn't handle." Alric frowned. "When we have time we'll have to break that habit. Never know when I might need to ride him. Storm Cloud will let you ride since he can smell my scent on your clothes." He hoisted his pack, leaving the stableman to care for the shaggy pack beast.

As they strode to the inn tension gathered in Kalia's gut. Five or six days travel was where the last report of the outlaws had arisen.

Alric arranged for a room and carried their packs to the second floor. Kalia sat at a table in the dining room and listened to gossip from the other diners. When Alric joined her and they ordered a full meal starting with soup and greens and ending with a fruit studded pudding and flaky sweet scones.

When they reached their room and undressed she touched the bracelet he wore on a chain. "Did your father give this to you?"

"He did."

Kalia stepped into his arms. "I have a tale for you about the matching one I wear." She told him the things her mother had related. She watched sadness fill his deep green eyes.

"My mother said her friend loved her bondmate. When her children were taken away by the Swordmaster she grieved and stepped into the abyss."

"He remained true to her until his death. I think I was the only reason he remained alive when he heard the news."

"Should we exchange the multi-link bracelet for the ones we now wear?"

"Not until you decide to declare our heart bonding in the salle."

"Will the day come? You know about the threats he has made."

"We have a year before a decision must be made." He settled on the bed. "We won't give your father a reason to carry out his threats. Do you think he reads the lines?"

Kalia frowned. "He sensed what Ilna did to me but he said he felt the power. I don't think he reads the lines." She slid beneath the linen sheet and turned to him.

Alric drew her into his arms. Their lips brushed. She felt the rise of desire and kissed her way down his chest and stroked his belly. His erection rose to meet her hand. She stroked the tip and felt a drip of fluid.

"Enough or I'll release."

Kalia laughed and pushed the sheet down. In the moonlight she saw his body. She ran her tongue over his chest and watched the lines of fire follow the touch.

Alric lifted her. "Take my rod into your channel and ride me."

The new way delighted her. As she moved he caressed her breasts and rolled the nipples. One of his hands slid between their bodies. He touched a spot sending a spear of fire shooting through her. He erupted. Her body tightened and exploded. She collapsed on his chest.

* * *

In the morning while they ate, a group of men arrived. Their rumpled clothing and newly healing wounds told her the men had encountered trouble. The three stood in the entrance. One of the group strode toward their table.

"Defender," he said. "There's trouble. Pack of men came to our farm."

"Outlaws?" Alric asked.

"Had to be."

"How many?"

"Didn't count the number. Was a pack. Some took our cattle and food from the storehouse. Slim pickings there, seeing harvest is months away. Four remained. Had their way with my wife and sister. Took my daughter."

"Where are the women?" Kalia asked.

"At the herb woman's."

A younger man glared. "One of the men wore a Defender's shirt. Had eyes as black as dead embers."

Petan, Kalia thought. How many men had he gathered? "How old is your daughter?"

"Fifteen and was to be chosen by the Defenders for training. She was quick to learn the sword and knife. Marked at least one of the men."

"When did this happen?" Alric asked.

"Been three days on the road but could take one or two if you're riding."

Alric waved to the innkeeper. "Feed these men

and give them a room." He turned to the three. "Rest before continuing your journey to the Guild House. Tell the Justicars what you've told me."

Kalia and Alric finished their food and went to the stable. While they saddled their steeds, Kalia met his gaze. "Do you think we'll find these outlaws?"

"I believe we will. Once the men reach the Hall and place a complaint with the Justicars, patrols will be sent out. We only have to locate the hiding place."

"What if the outlaws have prisoners?"

"We'll do what we can."

Alric helped her into the saddle. Kalia rode onto the road.

Chapter 13

With the directions he'd received from the farmers, Alric pushed the pace. He spotted the lane he believed led to the farm and signaled Kalia to follow with the pack beast. They passed newly planted fields and continued to the farmyard.

"Check the house," he called. "I'll look into the other buildings."

"What am I looking for?" she asked.

"See what they took. Was it just food they wanted or did they remove articles of value like clothes, jewelry and other goods?"

He dismounted and began his search. A few fowl scattered when he looked into the coop. The sty, the smoke house and the barn were empty. He noted several barn felines and one farm dog. Looked like the farm wagon had been taken.

Kalia left the house. "I believe they took everything of value, including blankets and quilts. I wonder how the patrol for this sector missed signs of these outlaws."

"By them staying hidden in the forest and not attacking anyone until the patrol passed," he said. "Maybe they have a source of information in the Hall. I'm sure there were also observers in the village where we stayed at an inn."

Alric stooped to examine a knife lying on the ground that showed evidence of a fight. The farmer had said his daughter had skills and would have been accepted as a Defender trainee. Why had the outlaws taken her? An idea he didn't like took form.

He signaled Kalia. "We need to move on. Nothing more can be discovered here."

"Which way do we go?"

He'd forgotten she'd never been on patrol. He beckoned. "Let me show you how to follow." He pointed to one of the bihorn's tracks. "See the notch in the right front shoe print. Means the animal's shoe has a flaw. Will show us the direction they rode." He also noticed this bihorn's tracks were deeper meaning either a huge rider of a double load.

Kalia pointed. "Looks like they went this way. Do you think we'll find them soon?"

Alric shook his head. "Not today. With luck this hoof print will show us where they have their camp. Remember the farmers were several days on the road."

For a time he followed the trail. He halted and held up a hand to stop Kalia. In the bushes he saw a body and moved closer to examine the wounds. The scruffy clothes and unshaven face told him the man, was the man the farmer's daughter had wounded.

He straightened, grabbed Storm Cloud's reins and continued forward until he reached the hard-packed surface of the road. He helped Kalia mount and checked the direction showed by the notched hoof. He swung into the saddle. When the sun moved to the west he spotted a campsite with a fire pit. A spring flowed into a stone basin.

He checked the area for signs of the men they sought. The ashes in the fire pit were cold and the telltale print of the hoof was absent. He notices signs a wagon and draft animals had been in the area. Perhaps the outlaws had divided into two groups.

"We'll camp here tonight." He dismounted and unloaded the pack beast.

Kalia joined him. "How far ahead do you think they are?"

"Don't know. The wagon stopped here but there are no signs of the ones we're seeking were here. They may have divided into two groups."

Kalia gathered the makings of a stew and placed the pot on the grill over the now lit fire. "I think Petan's one of them."

"Why?"

"Just seems like something he would do. If the girl really had Defender potential her lines would have been strong and he could leach them."

"You could be right."

"Will we rescue her before he drains her completely?"

Alric looked away. "I hope so but rescue is not why we're on the trail of these outlaws."

"I know. Find their camp and report." Kalia moved to face him. "Petan had two bondmates who died less than a year after the bonding."

Alric carried their blanket rolls to a spot beneath a giant oak. "I heard tales about bodies of women banished being found dead. Also those of young women who refused the training though they had been selected."

Kalia's lines of fire moved in an erratic pattern he recognized as fear. He reached for her hand.

"What can we do?" she asked.

"Move with caution." He ran a finger along her arm.

"What if we encounter Petan?"

"We'll observe. That's all we were ordered to do." He reached to stir the stew. "Though we haven't gone public with our heart bond I believe our status protects you from him."

Kalia edged closer. "I don't want to learn if you're right or wrong."

Alric clasped both her hands. He leaned forward and brushed her lips with his. Warmth flowed from the kiss in waves that caused him to harden. He rose, pulled her to her feet and kissed her with the urgency he felt.

"Come with me." He drew her toward the blankets. He drew her to the ground and savored her eager response. A need to mark her arose. He slid his lips over her skin and stroked her neck with his tongue. He sucked gently and then with more force. "I need you," he whispered.

"And I need you."

With a flurry of activity they undressed. Alric spread the blanket rolls and pulled her into his arms. She moved until she lay atop him. Her mouth fastened on his neck. Alric felt the draw and tightened his arms around her. He rolled her to her back and kissed his way down her body, stopping to lavish attention on her breasts.

Kalia's whimpers and small cries spurred him. He lifted her legs to his shoulders and found her mound. Her scent engulfed him. Her cries increased the working of his mouth and tongue on her labia.

"Alric, please, please."

"I'm trying."

"Join with me."

He lowered her legs and thrust inside. As her channel tightened around him, he wondered if he would ever grow tired of these moments. She moved. So did he. Heat burned through him and became volcanic. He spewed until he felt drained and collapsed on her.

"Love you," he gasped.

"Love you, too."

When his breathing returned to normal he rolled to his side. In the fading light of the sun he saw the red blotch on Kalia's neck. He rubbed his fingers over the area and though the lines flowed there, the mark remained a scarlet flame. He groaned.

"What?" Kalia asked.

"The mark on your neck."

"You have one, too. How odd. Though the lines gather I can't make the mark fade."

He laughed. "Wonder how long it will last."

"Guess we'll learn."

He reached for his clothes. "We'd better dress and prepare a meal. Then an early night. We must be off at dawn."

* * *

Glints of the light of dawn filtered through the leaves of the huge oak. Alric reached for his clothes and touched Kalia's shoulder. "Time to get ready to ride." He glanced at the mark on her neck and noticed it had remained the same bright scarlet color. Another thing they had to search for in the Archives.

Kalia moaned and opened her eyes. Her languid

stretch made him want to make love again but dawdling wasn't on the day's agenda.

They finished the stew from the previous night. Kalia drank three mugs of kafa and cleaned the things they'd used. Alric saddled Storm Cloud and started to load the pack beast.

A faint cry made him pause to listen. Was someone calling for help? He vaulted into the saddle. "Break camp. I think someone's in trouble." He flicked the reins.

"Be careful," Kalia cried. "Could be a trap."

Was she right? Alric pushed his bihorn into a gallop. The cries were louder. Did it matter if this was a trap? Defenders always answered cries for help. Storm Cloud raced around a bend and along a straight section of the road. Only the pounding of hooves against the dirt and the now louder cries of a woman filled Alric's ears. Sunlight blurred his vision. The tall spruces and bushy maples and oaks lining the road formed a green and brown tunnel.

As Storm Cloud rounded a second bend, Alric spotted a clearing. The screaming died. He focused on a scene that made him ill. Two men held a woman down while a third rocked above her. Chilling soprano laughter sounded. The third man bellowed his release. The lines of fire on the victim's skin were pale and thready. Had she been drained the way Kalia said the Swordmaster treated her mother.

As Alric leaped from his bihorn he drew his sword and knife. He raced toward the three. He slashed the arm of one of the men holding the woman still. The man yelled and grabbed his companion. The pair fled down the road. A pair of bihorns ran after them.

Alric turned to face the kneeling man. He leaped to his feet and pulled a sword free.

"Valdon." The name erupted in an angry roar. This man had nearly caused Alric's death. This time there would be no holding back for this was no duel, but a fight for justice. Alric whirled his sword and cut Valdon's shirt and marked his chest a half dozen times. The banished man backed away. Alric followed wielding his sword. He aimed for Valdon's knife hand and with a quick slice severed the hand from the wrist. Blood fountained. Valdon screamed and fell.

As Alric gulped deep breaths he heard the woman's laughter again. He stared. "Ilna, will you be next?"

"Not a chance. Take him."

Alric thought he heard Kalia scream. Impossible. He'd left her at their camp.

He whirled and evaded the whistling sword aimed at his back. "Petan." As Kalia had predicted this was an ambush. For a few moments they exchanged a flurry of blows. Alric moved aside to avoid a vicious thrust, caught his opponent's sword and missed seeing the hilt of a knife aimed at his head. He stumbled over Valdon's body and fell.

Alric struggled to roll away and got to his feet, but the body impeded him. His vision blurred. Something dark moved toward his head. A second blow connected. He fought descending darkness.

A trap. Kalia had been right. He had galloped to the rescue. Petan had won this time and maybe for all time. Aloud or in his thoughts the words rang.

* * *

Kalia watched Alric gallop away. All her instincts cried trap. Why hadn't he waited for her? Two stood a better chance than one, no matter how skilled he was with sword and knife.

While her thoughts churned, she grabbed the lead rope of the pack beast before the animal followed Storm Cloud. She tied the rope to a tree, saddled Mist and mounted.

How far ahead was her bondmate? As she sent Mist into a gallop the faint cries for help grew louder. What would she do when she reached the scene? Who knew how many outlaws they would face?

Thoughts of fighting roiled her gut. She wasn't a coward. Not long ago, she had faced Ilna in the circle. Meeting the outlaws wasn't like a duel in the salle. There were no rules and she would face desperate men.

Mist continued forward. Around a bend, down a straight, another bend, always pushing her steed for speed. As she neared the third bend, the scream stopped. How much longer before she reached the scene? Had Alric saved the woman or had she died?

Ahead, she saw Alric fighting a dark-haired man. Two others fled. A shout of encouragement to the man Alric fought startled Kalia. What was Ilna doing here?

Abruptly the fight ended in a spurt of blood. Alric's foe's hand flew from his body. He collapsed.

"Take him," Ilna shouted.

"Alric, beware!" Had he heard her? Had the

warning distracted him?

He wheeled and the sword Petan swung missed. For a short time they thrust and parried. Then Alric caught his opponent's sword and pushed it away.

"No," Kalia cried as the knife hit Alric's head and he stumbled over the bodies and fell.

Kalia slid from the saddle and ran to him. Petan aimed a booted foot and connected with Alric's head. Kalia reached her bondmate and lifted his head to her lap. The bleeding stopped. She touched his chest and felt the slow steady beat of his heart. She looked up to see Petan ready to plunge his sword into Alric's chest.

"Do it. Do it," Ilna chanted. "Kill him. Kill the man who was responsible for my banishment."

Kalia stared at Petan. "You killed him," she screamed. "What am I going to do? How can I live when he's dead?" She prayed Petan couldn't read the lines and would believe her frantic calls. Tears rolled down her face.

Petan lowered his sword. His laughter sent chills over her skin. "If anyone would know he's dead, you're the one. I know about your ability to read the lines. You should have rejected him and joined me." He glared. "You are mine."

Ilna ran to them and grabbed Petan's arm. "Kill her too. Kill her for me."

"Not a chance." He shook free and backhanded Ilna and set her flying to the ground. "Not a chance. She's my ticket back into the Hall. She's my way to prove my worthiness to the one who judges me."

Kalia lowered her gaze. "Worthy to whom?" She hadn't meant to speak aloud.

Petan grinned. "A powerful being you'll meet in time."

"What will you gain by returning me to the Hall?"

"Leadership of the Defenders." He reached for Ilna and grabbed her hair. "Though this git gifted Robec, he hasn't the inner strength to rule. The one I follow will reward me for helping him gain control of the Defenders."

Kalia frowned. What did he mean?

Petan released Ilna and grasped Kalia's arm. "Get up. You're coming with me."

She slid Alric's head from her lap. A puff of breath and a low moan emerged. "Why do you want me?" She raised her voice to cover Alric's sounds.

Ilna pounded Petan's back. "She can't have you. I'll be the new Swordmaster's bondmate."

He laughed. "I doubt Kalia will share."

Kalia stepped away from Alric and prayed he remain silent. She dare not let her captor know her bondmate lived. Regret rocked her thoughts. The intention of their assignment had been clear. Locate the hiding place of the outlaws and report what they found. At the moment failure loomed. Alric could turn defeat into victory but not now. He was in no condition to fight.

Petan pulled her away from the bodies. He tied her hands and feet before flinging her into the bihorn in front of the saddle. He mounted behind her.

"Where are you going?" Ilna asked.

"To the gathering place to see if those two fools who ran have arrived. If you're coming, I'm sure one of them will appreciate your talents."

Ilna grabbed the stirrup. "Help me up. I'll ride with you."

He kicked her away. "Too much weight. Take one of the other bihorns."

"Not his."

Storm Cloud stood over Alric's body. Did the animal know his master lived? Would that alert Petan? Kalia swallowed a sob. Ilna grasped Mist's reins and quickly mounted. The bihorn moved in a restless dance.

Kalia grimaced. Unless the other woman was an expert rider, Mist would throw her.

Petan chuckled. "She won't be with us for long. I know how your bihorn dislikes strangers."

Though she wanted to speak, her position kept her from drawing enough breath to force words out. Petan's bihorn moved forward. Kalia closed her eyes. She had to escape, but how?

Petan stroked Kalia's back. "You are mine. Your father will be pleased when he learns I have you and Alric is dead. The Swordmaster plans to see me as Robec's Right Hand. Won't happen. Your father's plans aren't mine or the one guiding me. Before long I'll challenge your father. The Swordmaster will die. The patrols will be forced to accept me and the Defenders will rule the Guilds and Investia."

A time of chaos faced them, Kalia thought. The patrols, the other Guilds, the people would suffer should his plans come to pass. Petan would face challenges. Hopefully, he would lose.

Would Alric regain consciousness before they were too far from here so he could give chase? He wasn't ready for a fight. She wanted to cry. For now she must tolerate Petan until she found a way to escape.

Mist raced past. Ilna screamed. The bihorn passed close enough to brush against Kalia.

"Watch it," Petan shouted.

Mist reared, came down and bucked. Ilna flew from the saddle and landed on the ground. Petan's steed shied. Kalia slid to the ground. She rolled to keep from being trampled.

Petan rode his steed away from the fallen and vaulted to the ground. He ran to Ilna and kicked her abdomen, chest and head. "Stupid git."

As blow after blow landed Ilna screamed. Kalia stared at the scene. She expected Ilna's lines of fire to vanish but the oddly pale lines remained.

The ebony shade of Petan's made Kalia shudder. What would happen if those lines solidified? As he approached her, she wanted to roll away but couldn't. Would she be his next victim?

He lifted her and tossed her on the bihorn. "She won't bother you again."

"Is she dead?"

"Who cares?" He prodded his steed into a walk. A short distance from Ilna's body the bihorn entered the forest.

Tears trickled over Kalia's face. Alric, she cried silently. Be all right. Come for me.

Chapter 14

Bright light shone in Alric's eyes. The glow vanished to return again. With caution he opened his lids and stared at clouds skimming across the sun. Past midday. Why was he lying on the road? He moved his hands across a body. Who was there? What had happened? He tried to rise. His head throbbed with the beat of a dozen large drums. Keeping his eyes closed he eased into a sitting position.

With care he slitted his eyes open and saw the aftermath of a fight. Near the trees he saw a bihorn grazing. Was that where he'd spent the night? Why had he slept so late? A face crystallized among the fragments of memory. Kalia. The shards of recollection began to spin in random patterns like the bits of glass in the viewing tubes children loved. With a hand he touched his head and found two places where blood crusted.

As he got to his knees he couldn't suppress a groan. Slowly he got to his feet and remained unmoving while the drumbeat became staccato and the wavering scenery slid into place. He stepped away from the bodies to reach the shade beneath a maple tree before turning to study the bodies in hopes his memories would knit.

Valdon. A young woman. Dead. His stomach lurched. He spewed the contents on the ground.

More memories fused. The girl, an untrained Defender had died before she reached the Hall. The cries for help. The ride. The witnessed rape and the fight. Two men in flight. Ilna's laughter and demands. Alric stared at the scene. Alone now except for the dead.

Petan's attack. Kalia had been right. Where was she? His thoughts drifted. The camp. He'd told her to remain there. Before searching for the outlaw's camp he needed to return for her.

He whistled for Storm Cloud. The bihorn arrived at his side. Alric searched the road and found his knife and sword. He used Valdon's shirt to clean some of the clotted blood from the blades. An urgency to return to the camp for his bondmate caused the drums in his head to slow their beat.

He climbed into the saddle and reached for his flask to slake his thirst. Empty. Kalia. He needed to find her. Though his head pounded and the bitter taste of vomit lingered, he pushed his steed into a gallop and retraced his ride to where he'd left her.

When the large oak came into view, a final shard fitted into pace. Kalia had followed him, had cried a warning and had stopped the bleeding from his head wound and more.

Her scream echoed through him. "You killed him. What am I going to do?"

But he wasn't dead and she hadn't been at the place where he'd awakened. He groaned. Petan had her. Though Alric wanted to turn and pursue the fleeing pair, they had been gone for hours. Caution was needed. Surely they had reached Petan's camp. He had to follow and rescue her. Then they would return to the Hall and report.

What about their supplies and the pack beast?

He pushed Storm Cloud for the final distance to the camp. He spotted the shaggy animal. Most of the supplies remained on the ground.

He knelt at the spring and gulped handfuls of water. He splashed his face and cared for his weapons. Selecting two sacks he gathered clothes for them both and filled the pack. The second, he filled with food, utensils and two pans. After rolling Kalia's blanket he fastened the packs to the saddle. He filled two flasks with water and mounted his bihorn.

While returning to where he had fought and lost to begin the search for the track of the bihorn with the notched shoe, he munched on trail bread and cheese. As long as daylight remained he believed he could discover where Petan had left the road. Alric prayed the banished Defender hadn't harmed Kalia.

He passed the bodies. Though they deserved a burial he couldn't stop to dig a grave. Around a bend in the road he saw a crumpled body. His heart thundered. As he drew closer he saw the color of the woman's hair. Not Kalia. Relief swamped him. Blood rushed from his head.

As he rode past he heard a faint cry. He dismounted and peered around Storm Cloud searching the trees along the sides of the road searching for another ambush. Seeing no one, he went to the body.

"Ilna." He knelt and studied her flickering lines of fire. Life lingered but soon would vanish. Both of her eyes were blackened. Blood oozed from her nose and her mouth. He placed a finger at her throat and felt a stuttering pulse. "What happened?"

"You're dead." Her voice barely rose above a

whisper.

"I'm not. Who did this?" Though he knew, he needed confirmation.

"Petan. He hit."

Alric drew a deep breath. "Did he beat you?"

"Yes. Bihorn threw. Kalia."

"Where is Petan? Where is Kalia?"

"He took."

Alric drew a shuddering breath. He dare not let the image of Kalia battered like Ilna stir the cauldron of his emotions. "Where?"

"Hut. Forest. Tonight. Stay. Go."

"Go where?"

"Away." She raised a hand and pointed.

Alric pushed hair from her face. "Can I help you?"

"Dying. Bleed inside."

"Do you need water?"

Laughter more like a cackle spilled from her mouth. "Dead. You. He thinks." She gasped for air.

Alric watched the lines of fire vanish from her skin. He rose and whistled for Storm Cloud. The bihorn brayed. Alric hurried toward the sound and found not only his steed but Mist. After gathering the reins of both he walked along the road in the direction Ilna had indicated and searched the edge for the notched shoe. When he found the place where Petan had entered the forest, Alric stopped to decide what to do.

Though he could ride the bihorn and follow the trail the noise would alert anyone listening. He led the steeds beyond the place where Petan had entered the forest and found a clearing with grass and water.

According to the map there was a crossroads ahead with an alternate approach to the Hall. He fastened Mist's reins to Storm Cloud's saddle.

After drinking from the spring and eating bread and cheese he patted his bihorn. "When I need you, I'll whistle."

He jogged back to the place where'd he'd seen the tracks made by the notched shoe. As he started along the narrow path he thought about Kalia. His lines of fire flowed to the tips of his fingers and pointed in the direction she had taken.

* * *

The jouncing walk of the bihorn coupled with enervating fear send Kalia wandering in a fugue state. The bihorn's halt jolted her into the present. Where were they? How long had they traveled? The canopy of leaves above the trail allowed little spots of light to dapple the ground.

Petan dismounted. She watched him walk to a spring and stoop to drink. Her dry throat prevented her from asking him to loosen her bonds and allow her to walk. Her arms felt numb and so did her legs. When he took a bite of something taken from his pack, pangs of hunger attacked.

Kalia fought to control the fury rolling like a forest fire through her body. The Swordmaster had planned to bind her to Petan. Did the older man understand the one he'd chosen for his daughter had plans crafted by some mysterious person Petan named as his master.

Escape. There had to be a way. Petan's

ruthlessness had always frightened her. Beneath her anger embers of fear threatened to flare and burn all her thoughts away. Petan would do anything to bring his plans to fruition.

He approached the bihorn and dusted crumbs from his hands. "Time to move on. Another hour will see us to our destination." He mounted behind her.

"Water," she croaked.

He ran his hand over her back and rear. "Afraid not, my love. Be patient. You will receive all you deserve."

She shuddered beneath his touch.

He laughed. "No reason to fear. You'll enjoy the things I do to you. Hope you're as strong as your mother has been. I would hate to lose you but you do have a sister."

Doesn't he know Lasara has run away? Had the Swordmaster hidden this from his cohort?

Tremors shook her body. Alric, she cried silently. Come soon.

The darkness of the forest enclosed them in gloom. Though the sun still ruled the sky, the thick canopy of leaves shielded them from most of the light. She peered at the ground and saw they followed a path just wide enough for the bihorn. If her hands had been free, she would have torn cloth from her skirt to leave a trail for Alric. Once a briar scratched her arm and tore a piece from her sleeve. Was the scrap large enough for him to see? Though the thorns clutched her divided skirt she doubted they could tear the deerskin.

Alric. His name thundered in her thoughts. Had she been wrong about him? Was he alive? Calmness stilled her jangled fears. A smile formed. She had stopped the flow of blood. If he'd been dead the bleeding would have stopped. For once Petan had been a fool. He had believed her cries about the death of her bondmate.

Suddenly the calm vanished. Had Alric recovered from the blows to his head? Head wounds often stole the injured person's memories. She dare not think he wouldn't remember who he was and the reason for their mission. Could he save her? How many men waited at Petan's destination?

Could the gang of outlaws number more than the size of a patrol? Two had run from the fight. When she and Alric had searched the farm he had estimated at least five men had driven the livestock and perhaps another two of three had driven the wagon of loot. Alric could defeat two, even if Petan was one of the duelers, especially if Alric's presence shocked Petan.

Still, if she found an opportunity, she would run.

The jolting pace grew more uncomfortable. Though her arms had been bound to the front, the weight of her body numbed them. She felt as if her feet were lead weights. How soon would they reach their destination? Would he release the ropes when they did?

The trees thinned. The late afternoon sun shone on a clearing.

Petan halted the bihorn. He dismounted and pulled Kalia to the ground. She crumpled in a heap. He stood over her. His leer raised her anger. He bent and lifted her over his shoulder. He carried her to the hut she'd caught a glimpse of as she fell. He kicked the door open and dropped her on a cot against a side wall.

Two men lounged before the fireplace. The aroma of cooking meat and of kafa made Kalia's stomach rumble. Petan sliced the ropes on her hands and feet.

The men jumped to their feet. "Where's Ilna?" one asked. "I have a need."

"Dead," Petan said.

"Then this one's ours." A bearded man stepped to the cot and caressed Kalia's face. "Once you're done with her, that is."

Petan pushed the man aside. "She's not for you. She's mine until the Master decides if he wants her. Go see to my steed and take your time returning."

The men grumbled and cursed. Once the door closed behind them, Petan strode to Kalia and stared.

She bit her lip to hide the pain of returning blood to her arms and legs. She wouldn't scream though this took all she could muster as the prickles turned into ribbons of pain.

He stalked away and lifted a jug. He poured liquid, tossed the contents of the mug back and filled the container again. He sat on the cot beside her and held the cup to her lips. "Drink. Will help."

Kalia gulped a mouthful of the pungent beverage. A fiery trail burned from her mouth to her gut. She pushed his hand away. "No more." Whatever she'd drunk made her head and the room spin. Her stomach lurched and she swallowed several times to keep from being sick.

He laughed, lifted the mug and drained the remainder. "Frumenti. You'll learn to like the rush of energy this brings. Master provides a constant supply.

Your mother drinks this when she visits your father. Makes his taking of her donation easier."

Kalia rubbed her arms. "I'm not my mother."

"So I know." He frowned. "Who removed the power from your lines or did Ilna lie about the gifting?"

Kalia turned her head away. She wouldn't speak of Alric. "Why did she try to harm me?"

"She figured since she couldn't reach Alric she'd infuse you and you would pass the power to him." A sneer curved his mouth. "Stupid git. Didn't know the power doesn't work that way. Master punished her."

"How do you know it's gone?" The longer she kept him talking the more she would recover and find a way to escape.

He grasped her arm. "I don't feel the power surging through you. Tell me what happened."

Kalia clamped her lips in a firm line. She wouldn't answer him. The initial impact of the beverage vanished. Her head cleared. Her arms and legs no longer tingled or hurt. She needed to wait for an opening. Though she studied his lines she couldn't detect his moves.

With a serpent-like move he grasped the neck of her shirt. He knelt with his knees on either side of her hips. He raised her arms above her head. Dark lines of fire gathered around his mouth. His lips touched the spot on her neck where Alric had marked her. Revulsion filled her.

Petan reared back as though he'd been shocked. He touched the mark with a finger. "How could you? You're mine. My mark belongs there, not his."

"Why?"

He released her hands. She waited for a blow.

"You're heart bound. Impossible. He's dead."

"Is he?"

Petan rose. "Then we'll do this the hard way. When I'm done I'll give you to my friends. They'll take you like they did the girl."

Petan lowered his head. His mouth ground against hers and he forced his tongue over her teeth. She bit. The taste of blood filled her senses. He hollered and pulled away. He aimed his fist at her face but she rolled from the cot. Kalia pulled the knife he'd forgotten to remove. With a quick jab she slammed the blade into his thigh and twisted. She inched away from him. He bellowed and reached for her braid.

Kalia scrambled across the floor. She tried to read his lines.

He pulled the knife free and threw. The point stuck in the floor inches from her.

"Stupid git."

The door opened. His cohorts burst into the room. "We want our piece of her," one shouted.

"Like it when they fight," the other drawled.

"She's mine," Petan shouted. He moved toward Kalia.

Instead of diving for her, the men tackled Petan. They met in a tangle of fists and feet. Their curses filled the air.

Kalia crawled away. Once she crossed the threshold she rose and ran. The sun was near setting and she welcomed the coming twilight, a prelude to night. The sound of the fight carried to her even after she reached the shelter of the trees. She found a narrow trail and hoped this was the one Petan had used, the one to lead her to the road and Alric.

Her breath came in gasps as she plunged along the path. When her sides heaved and pains cramped her legs, she halted with her back against a tree to rest until her breathing quieted. If Petan followed, she didn't want to give her location away.

Alric, where are you? Her eyes narrowed to watch the movement of her lines. What had he told her? The time she'd run away he'd used his thoughts and his lines to find her.

She pushed away from the tree and slowly made her way along the path, allowing her sight to adjust to the increasing darkness.

She was free and intended to remain that way. With luck she would reach the road, find Mist and seek Alric. She moved forward, pausing every ten steps to listen for followers. The activity of the day and the anger she'd felt brought exhaustion. She wasn't sure she could continue. She halted and examined the surrounding trees seeking one she could climb and shelter for the night.

Chapter 15

Alric made his way along the narrow trail. If he hadn't used his lines of fire to direct him toward Kalia, he would have believed this was a random animal path. He stopped at a spring and drank before moving on. As he studied the moist ground he noticed the notched shoe mark and knew he was heading in the right direction. Insects crawled over a heel of bread carrying bits back to their nest. How long ago had Petan and Kalia stopped here?

Through the dense canopy he caught glimpses of the sky and saw the sun moved toward setting. How many men would he encounter at the end of the journey? Petan plus the two who had run? Could there be more? The men driving the stolen livestock and those driving the cart had stayed at the spring where he and Kalia had stopped. The tracks he recognized had been absent. Would he have to fight an entire band or could he find a way to steal Kalia away?

As he continued, he passed clumps of briars. On one thorn he spotted a scrap of green cloth. The material held traces of Kalia's scent. A smile formed. Even though he trusted the lines, this was evidence he moved toward her.

Occasionally, a breeze lifted the leaves to show the now graying twilight sky. He thought of Kalia and followed in the direction shown by the lines.

Concern flooded his thoughts. Was Kalia safe? Would their heart bond protect her from Petan's savage nature?

He stiffened. A cracking noise burst through the soft rustle of the leaves. Someone or something approached. He slipped from the path and hid behind a tree with limbs low enough to climb if necessary. After unsheathing his knife he peered into the darkness and saw movement. As the figure drew closer, he waited.

Once the person passed his hiding place he caught Kalia's scent. He slipped behind and covered her mouth with his hand. He sensed the flicker of fear and anger. Their lines of fire flared. Alric put his lips against her ear. "You're safe."

She slumped against him. "We must hurry. He'll come to find me and this is no place for a duel."

He turned her to face him and pressed his mouth to hers. He deepened the kiss hoping to give and receive strength. "Give me a moment to locate our steeds. I left them in a site away from the place where Ilna died." He visualized Storm Cloud. Would the trick of the lines work with the steed as well as with Kalia?

"What are you doing?"

Her question broke his concentration. "Finding a direction by thinking of my steed." He formed the picture again and watched the lines of fire. "This way."

"Let me try." Moments later, she laughed. "My lines point in the same direction."

Since her attempt matched his, Alric clasped her hand. He led her from the trail and into the trees. Their new path took them in random directions with twists and turns around trees. "When we reach the road we should be close to our bihorns. If I don't spot Storm Cloud at once I'll whistle. I've trained him to come at my call."

For a moment she leaned against him. "I must learn how to call Mist that way." She stepped back. "Petan said some things that puzzled me."

"You can tell me later. We need to move through this tangle, find the steeds and ride away from here as fast and as long as we can. Come dawn we'll find shelter, sleep through the day and travel at night. Once we reach the Hall, I hope we can convince the Swordmaster to send a force to find Petan and his gang."

"Do you think he will?"

"If not, he'll be challenged," Alric said.

"Will he send them out if Lasara's searchers haven't returned?"

"That would give him an excuse. Let's hope they have."

Alric moved forward, pausing to check his lines every time they had to travel around an obstacle. He felt confident their trail would remain hidden from any pursuer until morning.

As the trees thinned Alric saw the star-lit sky. The road was near. He whistled and hoped Storm Cloud heard. The welcome sound of a bray brought a laugh of relief. He pulled Kalia toward the sound. Before long the bihorns appeared.

Kalia pulled her hand free and ran to her steed. The animal lipped her hair. Kalia laughed and rubbed the steed between the horns.

Alric strode over and assisted her into the saddle. "I've your blanket, a sack with clothes and one with food." He transferred the blanket and clothes to her steed.

"What about the pack beast?" she asked.

"Freed the animal and left it with the rest of our supplies. The beast will either return to the Hall or some farmer will gain an animal." He mounted Storm Cloud. "Let's ride." He chose to continue east at a steady pace. When they reached the crossroads he chose the south fork.

Kalia caught up to him. "Why this road? Shouldn't we retrace the route we took to arrive here?"

"The map shows this road will join another turning toward the Hall. This area appears to be sparsely settled. Petan would hear about our passing if we backtracked. Imagine he has spies in the village where we stayed. That allowed him to set his trap."

"Then we must avoid people."

"If possible." He prodded Storm Cloud into a gallop and heard the pounding of hooves behind him.

As the sky lightened Alric searched the road on either side for a place to camp for the day. He spotted a barn in an overgrown field. He turned his steed into the lane where weeds and brush had taken root. The barn held none of the comforts of the one where they'd spent their first night. Three walls and part of a roof remained. The important thing was they couldn't be seen from the road.

Once they unsaddled their mounts, Alric tackled the pump and finally coaxed a stream of water to flow. Though rusty at first, the liquid cleared. He cut a small fire pit and lit dry wood in the narrow hole. After heating water for kafa he set dried meat and vegetables to cook.

"Aren't you afraid someone will see the smoke?" she asked.

"As you see, there's little. The fire will die and we'll have warm stew when we wake. Be sparing with the kafa so there's some left for your wake up."

She poured most of the beverage into her empty flask. "I'll save this until then."

Alric handed her trail bread and cheese. "Good thought."

She laughed. "I'll need to be alert for the ride. Do you think we'll return safely? I'm sure he's searching."

He sipped from a mug of water. "We will. Tell me what Petan said to trouble you."

Kalia moved closer. He slid his arm around her shoulders.

"He gave me this vile drink called frumenti." She shuddered. "He said my mother drinks this when she visits the Swordmaster. Petan said it helps her when he takes her donation."

Alric frowned. "Must be some kind of drug."

"The worst thing he said was that his master provided the drink. I fear he means someone like the sorcerers our people fled."

Alric drew a deep breath. "I hope you're wrong."

"If one of them found a way to cross the mists we'll face disaster."

"Only if more than one braved the barrier. All the old tales said they worked in groups."

She pressed against him. "I wonder if the Swordmaster knows of this master or is Petan the only one."

"I'm not about to ask." Alric finished his share of the food. "When we return, we should search the Archives for more information."

"Good idea." She yawned. "How will we enter the Hall? Do you think using the gate is wise?"

"We'll leave the bihorns in the pasture and climb the wall."

"No need to do that. I know of a secret entrance into the tunnel. Then there's a hidden passage in the stable wall. Since we're going at night, we can reach our wing in secret."

He nodded. "Sounds like a plan. Three more nights should see us to the Hall." He stretched on his blanket and pulled her into his arms. Before long he knew she slept. He wasn't far behind.

* * *

On the morning after the third night of travel, they camped in a small copse beside a rushing stream. A waterfall tumbled over rocks into a pool before flowing on its way.

Tonight they would ride to the Hall. They should arrive several hours after nightfall.

Alric set a fire in the pit and brewed kafa and cooked the remainder of the mixed grains. Kalia unrolled their blankets beneath a flowering willow tree where a sweet scent filled the air.

Alric dished out the stew and filled Kalia's mug with kafa. "There'll be enough powder to steep a pot while we sleep." He grinned. "As soon as I've eaten

I'm going to bathe. Join me. Storm Cloud will warn us if there's danger."

Kalia scraped her bowl. "You've trained him to do more things than most bihorns."

"Was worth the trouble."

When he finished eating he entered the bower and gathered clothes and a drying cloth. He undressed and walked to the pool. The grass cushioned his bare feet. At the bank he dove into the water. The chill invigorated him.

A wave engulfed him. "Cold," Kalia said.

He paddled to her side and ran his tongue over her lips. "I'll warm you." And when she accepted his embrace, the part of him shriveled by the cold water recovered.

She pressed against him. "I'm sure you can." She circled his neck with her arms and set her tongue into an exploration of his mouth.

Alric savored the taste of kafa. He cupped her buttocks and pulled her against his rod. Her nipples beaded against his chest. He drew back to gulp a breath.

"We need to wash," she said. "We've been days with quick sponges. Soap's on the bank. Race you there."

He embraced the challenge and reached the soap first. He dipped it into the water and slicked his hands. After giving her the small piece, he washed the smooth skin of her back. He took the soap again and moved to lave her breasts. He liked the way her eyes glowed with passion. When his hands moved over her belly, her gasp made his erection throb. He slid his soapy hand into her treasure spot and heard her sighs change to moans.

His body tensed. Her mouth pressed to his and he swallowed her cries. She ducked into the water and came up behind him.

"My turn."

As her hands moved over his back, tendrils of heat made Alric feel he stood in a steam bath. She ran her hands over his buttocks and slid one between his thighs to stroke his sac. As she moved around him she slid her soaped hands over his chest and down to caress his erection.

"Enough or all will be too soon ended." He pulled her close and lifted her so his rod nudged between her legs. She arched back allowing him to enter her. Then she straightened and clasped her arms around his neck. As Alric kissed her lightly, he walked to where the stream cut into the bank. He carried her to their bower.

* * *

Kalia's breath came in short pants. Though she wanted to move, Alric's hands held her still. Each step he took sent small arrows of heat through her body. They reached the bower and the sweet perfume of the pale flowers added urgency to the sensual bliss beckoning.

Alric caught her lower lip with his teeth. He leaned against the willow and slowly lowered them to the blankets. As he inched lower the movement of his tongue in her mouth ignited a need to move.

She lay atop him. His hard member filled her

channel. Their tongues thrust in harmony and the tendrils of fire flowed from mouth to her core. Her knees pressed against the blanket. She began to move and so did he, his hips thrusting in a steady pattern that carried her higher and higher. Her moans changed to one long cry, echoed by his deeper growl. Urgency filled her and the sound of flesh slapping flesh caused her to clench her inner muscles as she exploded and felt him erupt.

She collapsed against his chest. Her breaths came in shuddering gulps. Once she could speak, she raised her head and stared into his eyes. "We must declare we are bonded forever."

"Soon." We need to visit the Archives and learn more about the past. I only hope there's time." He rolled to his side and pulled her into a tight embrace. "Sleep now. At dusk we must ride the final leg of our journey."

Kalia snuggled against him. She had his heart as he had hers. She only hoped Petan didn't return to ruin the bonding.

* * *

Kalia lay in Alric's arms. Her head pressed against his chest. The beat of his heart soothed her. She opened an eye and saw the sun had moved far to the west. As soon as night fell they would be on their way to the Hall.

He groaned and stretched. "Kalia."

She shifted position. "I'm awake. When we reach the Hall, where will we go?"

"To Sando first. If he won't challenge your father we'll seek someone else who will."

"Who?"

"Do you think Robec will?"

Apprehension gathered in her gut. How could she explain the way dueling had escalated her anger and made the darkness grow? "He's tainted. Think of my lines when I returned from the duel with Ilna. He could become as evil as the Swordmaster and Petan have."

Alric growled. "Who then?"

"You."

"I have no desire to be the leader. I have no training in leadership. I'm a simple Defender who is successful as a dueler."

She pressed against him. "You're more. No matter how badly you've been treated you haven't given up."

Alric drew a deep breath. "Because of the promises I made to my father on the day he died. To find my sibs. To become a Defender. To return them to the old ways. I don't know what those ways are."

She pressed her lips to his. "We can learn by searching the records in the Archives." She tightened her arms around him. "You are the best one, for you want no power for yourself."

* * *

At dusk they saddled their mounts and rode from what for a time had been a place of enchantment. Kalia wished they could have remained longer but duty called. There were outlaws to discover and drive from the land and to learn what Petan and the one he called his master had planned. Could they? The question troubled her. She wasn't sure they could but she dare not let her unsettled thoughts flow free.

A few hours of travel brought them to the pasture where most of the Defender's bihorns grazed. They unsaddled their steeds and hid their gear beneath a stand of thorn bushes.

This done, they set off at a brisk walk toward the dark looming walls surrounding the Guild House. When they reached their destination Kalia ran her hand along the rough surface of the stones until she found the catch. She pressed a single stone and breathed a sigh of relief when the segment of thinner stone swung out.

Alric entered first. She followed. The opening closed cloaking them in darkness.

"Walk with your left hand on the stone wall," she said. "When you reach a place where you can go no further, I'll find the catch."

"A lantern would help," he said.

"We don't have one, so move." She placed one hand on his back and nudged him forward.

When they emerged into the tunnel connecting the Halls of the Guild House, Kalia opened a secret passage through the rear wall of the stable. Once again they used the wall as a guide. They emerged in the courtyard.

Alric halted to study their surroundings. Clouds scudded across the moon causing shadows and light to fall in erratic patterns. "Why the hidden passages?" he asked.

Kalia turned. "I don't know. They were built

when the Guild House was erected. Maybe as an escape if enemies should arrive."

He clasped her hand. They scurried toward the wing of the Hall where Sando's patrol was housed. Inside, Alric led her past four doors before opening one and ushering her into a sitting room. "Wait here. I'll rouse Sando."

Kalia remained pressed against the door. While they had crossed the courtyard, she had seen several shadowy figures. Had she and Alric escaped notice? The random glints of moonlight could have revealed their movements. She heard a murmur of voices.

Sando entered carrying a lit lamp. He placed the lantern on a table. "Why creep in at night?"

"Sit," Alric said. "The outlaws are a greater threat than we thought. I'll begin the story and Kalia will give the ending." He began at the inn and the arrival of the farmers and continued to the fight and Petan's attack.

Kalia took over. "In one thing Petan failed. He believed my cries of Alric's death. That was fortunate." She spoke of Ilna's fall when her steed bucked. Petan's attack of the younger woman, the forest hut and then of the things Petan had said.

"We'll tell the Swordmaster," Sando said.

Kalia shuddered. "He'll do nothing. Petan visits him. They bear the same sullied lines. Someone must challenge him."

Sando shook his head. "I'm not good enough with sword and knife to defeat your father. Robec is the logical choice."

"For two reasons that isn't a good idea. Robec's

lines are tainted. Robec would easily be defeated by the Swordmaster. With no heir, he could put my mother aside."

Sando frowned. "How do you know he would?"

"He has threatened to do this if I refuse to break the bond with Alric."

"And the lines. How do you know they're sullied?"

Alric leaned forward. "I can read his lines and I have seen the darkness."

"So can I," Kalia said.

Sando clasped Alric's arm. "You must be the challenger. None of the patrol leaders will. When will you call him out?"

"I would rather not do this," Alric said.

Kalia stared into Alric's eyes. "He's right. You are the only one who could defeat him."

Alric groaned. "Tomorrow after the nooning. Until then we must remain apart from everyone." He squeezed Kalia's fingers. "She needs a map of the Hall to show you some hidden passages. They should be watched lest Petan creep inside."

Sando nodded. "Let me dig one out." He opened a chest and pulled out a roll. "This should be the one. You mark while I consider where to hide you."

"Why not in Alric's suite?" Kalia asked.

"Your father has set a watcher there."

Kalia scowled. "What does he hope to find?" She opened the roll and began to mark the passages she knew.

When she finished Sando led them to a room on the second floor. "Listen for my special knock. I'll bring clean clothes and kafa while we lay plans for our meeting with the Swordmaster."

Once he left, Kalia entered the necessary and washed before joining Alric on the wide bed. She wished she could see her mother. What would the Swordmaster's death do to the older woman? Though Alric would aim for a bloodless victory, the leader of the Defenders would fight to the death.

Chapter 16

Alric woke Kalia with kisses. She turned on her side and ran her hands over his chest. As he explored her mouth, he deepened the kiss. His rod thickened and grew firm. He left her mouth and kissed a leisurely path toward her breasts.

A series of three raps followed by one made him growl. "Later."

"Definitely." She scrambled from the bed and grabbed her clothes before entering the necessary.

Alric pulled on trousers and went to the door. "Sando."

"Who else? Change of plans."

"Why?"

"Swordmaster knows you're here."

Alric widened the opening to take a pitcher of kafa from the patrol leader. "Who told him?"

"Who knows? The man sets patrol spying on patrol. Heard a stir at the gate last night. Most of the searchers are back."

"Lasara?"

"Not found."

Kalia reached around Alric and grasped the pitcher. She filled a mug with the steaming aromatic brew. "What will we do now?"

"Come to the baths with the patrol, then to the morning meal. After that several of us will accompany you to the meeting. We'll wait for you at the foot of the stairs."

"Five minutes." Alric dashed into the sleeping chamber for the rest of his clothing.

As soon as he pulled on his shirt and vest, Kalia handed him a mug of kafa. "Sorry it isn't citren."

"I'll have some soon enough." He drained the mug and grasped the record book, the only thing he brought from his pack. He opened the door. "Shall we?"

"As if we have a choice." Kalia set the mug on a table and followed him into the hall. "Bathing in hot water will be a treat."

"But not as much fun as the stream."

Kalia halted and turned back. "I forgot my weapons." She re-entered the suite and returned with her knife and sword. "Will wearing them ever become a habit?"

Alric clasped her hand. "Soon enough."

As they strode along the corridor, to the stairs he glanced at the few closed doors and the many open ones. The closed ones belonged to patrol members who were riding one of the quadrants. The empty ones told of the decline of the Defenders. In the years since he'd begun his training, the population had decreased. Fewer candidates arrived from the villages and farms. Failed bondings and few births added to the decline.

The patrol members waited at the foot of the stairs. Kalia joined the women and Alric walked with the men.

Though he and Kalia had bathed in the stream, Alric welcomed the steaming water. Muscles stiff from nights of riding and remaining from the fight with Valdon and Petan loosened as heat infused and banished the stiffness. He scrubbed and washed his hair. For a time he lingered until the kinks completely uncoiled. He needed a supple body to face the coming challenge.

Would the Swordmaster's Seconds stand with him? Would they step aside and let their leader fight alone? Alric planned strategies for each of the possibilities.

He swam to the warm rinsing pool and then took a quick plunge into the frigid one to wash away all traces of sleep. After drying his hair, gently touching the places where Petan had bashed him with knife and boot, he grabbed clean clothes. He joined his friends to leave the room.

Sando clapped his shoulder? "Ready?"

"As much as I can be."

The older man whistled. "Line up. Let's join our ladies."

Ganor stood at Alric's side. "If one or both of the Seconds join the Swordmaster I'll stand at your side."

"So will I," Sando said.

"Thanks."

The door of the women's bathing room opened. Kalia followed the other women and came to Alric's side. The sixteen men and women marched to the refectory. Alric introduced her to the patrol members she hadn't met.

As they choose food to break their fast, Kalia stared at Alric's selections. "Why are you eating so hearty? What about the duel?"

"That won't happen until this afternoon." He

slid a plate of eggs and smoked shoat plus one of hot grain cakes onto his tray.

"How do you know?"

"We've been summoned to present our report to the Swordmaster. Sando, Ganor and their mates will go with us."

Kalia's hands shook. The plates on her tray rattled. "What does he want? Do you think he knows about our bond?"

"He might but that won't be his focus. Our report about Petan and the outlaws will anger him."

Kalia's body shook. "Do I have to go?"

"There's nothing to fear."

"You don't know him. He could order us banished or worse." She placed her tray on the table where the rest of the patrol had gathered.

Alric leaned forward and spoke to Sando. The laughter and chatter of the others covered their low-voiced plans for the coming challenge.

"When you visit the Swordmaster in his office, present your report," Sando said. "Answer his questions and try not to argue if he disagrees."

Kalia scowled. "He'll argue. He won't believe Petan has anything to do with the outlaws, even if we had witnesses who would identify the Swordmaster's favorite."

"What he says won't change what we know," Ganor said. "The Justicars have received a complaint. How he feels won't matter when Alric wins the challenge."

Alric leaned forward. "Will the leaders of the other Guilds be present? The duel won't be official if they aren't."

Sando lifted his fork. "The Swordmaster summoned them. Said the witness was needed."

Alric tapped his fork on the table. Something about that seemed wrong. How could the Swordmaster know he would face a challenge? He attacked his food. When he swallowed the last bite and drained the mugs of citren, he reached for Kalia's hand. "Are you finished?"

She nodded. "Couldn't eat any more."

Sando rose and gestured to his mate and Ganor. "Ready?"

"Yes."

The six walked along the corridor to the Swordmaster's office. No matter what the man demanded, Alric wouldn't let Kalia break their bond.

Sando knocked on the door and in response to the summons turned the knob and prepared to enter. He and Ganor flanked Alric. The women did the same for Kalia.

Kalia's mother pushed past them. Tears flowed over her cheeks. Kalia turned to follow.

"You can't leave yet," Alric whispered. "When we're finished here I'll go to the Women's Quarters with you."

"So will I," Sando's bondmate said.

Rila touched Kalia's hand. "I'll come, too."

The women followed the men inside. "Alric and Kalia reporting. Our assignment was to discover the location of the outlaws plaguing the eastern sector."

The Swordmaster glared. "Who ordered this assignment?"

Sando stepped forward. "Since you were concerned with your missing daughter, when complaints reached the Justicars and my patrol wasn't sent on the search, I ordered Alric and Kalia to investigate."

Alric stepped to the desk. "This is the report of our trip."

The Swordmaster opened the book and glanced at the pages. He returned the journal to Alric. "We'll discuss this matter another time. Kalia, the time has come for you to keep your promise."

"I see," she said. "Remind me of what I said and of my free will in speaking, not the control you influenced on my words."

He stalked from behind the desk and clasped her hand. "Speak the words you must say."

She shook her head. "Those words weren't mine and you have no power to force them. Lasara is gone. Robec is hiding."

"But your mother?"

Alric laughed. "Are you planning to put her aside? She is heart bound to you. Don't you know of the penalties for breaking one? Unlike the woman you tried to force to break her bond by banishing her mate and stealing her children, your bondmate will live. You may not."

"Your father was warned not to speak of that."

"And he didn't. He died keeping your secret. Other people weren't warned." Alric thought he saw a hint of remorse in the other man's eyes. "The man you selected as your son's Right Hand has gone rogue. Valdon and Ilna are dead. Beware Petan. He wants to take your place."

"And you don't?"

Alric shrugged. "Believe what you will. I have no desire to lead. But for the promise I made to my father before he died, I wouldn't be here."

* * *

Kalia squeezed Alric's hand. They had done their best to sway the Swordmaster from his stubborn adherence to his plan for Alric. Her bondmate's lines of fire settled into a smooth pattern of movement. Relief caused her to feel faint. She leaned against Alric. Swooning would bring an accusation from the leader of the Defenders. Would he challenge Alric outside the salle? The possibility chilled her.

She stared at the turgid lines on the leader's skin. "Are you finished with me?" she asked. "You've seen our report. The assignment discovered a possible location of the outlaws."

The Swordmaster returned to the chair behind the desk. "I've more important matters facing me. When the gong calls you to the salle, don't consider fleeing. The gate guards have their orders. Anyone can enter but none can leave."

Kalia lowered her gaze. Anyone can enter. His knowing smirk convinced her he wanted the man he considered his ally to be present.

"Dismissed."

His barked order diverted her thoughts. She backed to the door. The others joined her in the hall. Kalia slumped against the wall.

Sando paused. "After you visit your mother, come to my suite. We have plans to make." He took his bondmate's hand. "We'll wait and discuss what we know and what we've learned."

Alric nodded. "Send men to check the secret entrances and the ways Kalia marked."

"Will do."

Rila walked beside Kalia. Ganor and Alric followed. At the door of the Women's Quarters Kalia turned. "Just Rila." She knew her mother would never confide her pain if the men were there.

"We'll wait here," Alric said.

Rila and Kalia entered the lounge and hurried down the hall leading to the sleeping chambers. Sounds of sobbing filtered from her mother's room. Kalia burst inside. "Mother, what did he do?"

"He. He will break our bond. Does he realize what will happen when he claims another mate? He will be banished. I'm his third."

"Are you sure?"

"Yes. He believes his position as Swordmaster will allow him to do as he wants."

"You must keep him from making the declaration." Kalia grasped her mother's hand. "How can he believe he will succeed?"

"I don't think he cares. He's driven by those tainted lines. So is your brother but Robec fights against their control."

Rila knelt beside the chair. "There's something other than banishment to fear. I am heart bound to Ganor. Before he declared for me he had an interest in another young woman who liked to flirt and had a train of men. Ganor wanted to break our bond and claim her but illness struck him. The Healers found no cure. Only through my touch did he recover. He bound his heart to me. When the bell chimes you must be in the salle lest he becomes sick and dies."

"He forbade my presence."

"A heart bound woman dare not stay away."

"Mother, listen to her." Kalia kissed her mother's cheek.

The older woman covered her face with her hands. "So if I don't go he might die?"

"Yes," Rila said.

Kalia's shoulder muscles tightened. Could her mother buck years of obedience to the Swordmaster's demands? "Say you will be there."

"I will creep into the hall." Kalia's mother wiped her eyes. "When he demanded the bracelet I couldn't remove it. He tried but the clasp seemed fused. He intends to send for someone from the Artisans to cut the clasp." She rose. "I must hide."

Kalia embraced her mother. "A question. How long has the Swordmaster been so angry and cruel?"

"Began when Alron returned from an assignment where he found the bracelets of many metals. Your father wanted them but his friend refused. Instead Alron used them to bond with his chosen and they made their bond a forever one."

"Were the Swordmaster's lines smudged then?"

Her mother frowned. "That happened after our children were born. That boy came. Alron wanted Petan to be fostered. Your father disagreed. There was a duel over that and because your father wanted Alron's bondmate. Your grandfather was angry when Robar lost. He found a way to banish Alron."

Questions needing answers flowed through Kalia's thoughts. What did the bracelets signify? Was there time to search the Archives before the meeting?

She rose and embraced her mother. "I'll see you in the salle."

"Will you find Lasara and care for Robec? He sickens like your father."

"I know. There is a cure. I was tainted but the double heart bond with Alric was the answer."

Her mother gasped. "So simple yet so hard."

"I know." Kalia walked to the door.

Rila followed her. When they reached the hall, Alric and Ganor leaned against the wall. Kalia told them what her mother had said. "We need to know more about those bracelets, the bonds and the Defenders."

Alric nodded. "There's time to discover a bit before the nooning." He motioned to Ganor. "Tell Sando we'll see him in the refectory. There are things we must research in the Archives."

"Take care."

Once they reached the room where the records were kept, Kalia lit several lamps and carried them to the rear of the room. There, she slid aside a tapestry to reveal another room with books and scrolls. She set the lanterns on a small table and pulled aside another tapestry to reveal a window. Sunlight brightened the room.

"I never knew this was here," Alric said.

"Few people do. These are the oldest records. I

haven't touched the scrolls but the books might tell us some of the things we need to know." She selected several leather bound volumes. "The pages are fragile and the words faded."

"We need to know so many things," Alric said. "Where should we begin?"

"The special bracelet, I think. If we can learn what they mean we'll know what we should do next. If there's time we can read about the lines." Kalia passed one of the books to him.

Alric set the chairs so the lanterns and sunlight could aid their reading. For a time, he carefully turned pages and peered at the fading lines.

He straightened. "Not about the bracelets but this is of interest. Three men have been infected by the sorcerers. They crossed the mists with us. They have been … the following words are too faded to read." He glanced at Kalia. "The cure was found yet one died. The other two have recovered. Thus we suggest … Again the words can't be read. Maybe with more light we could."

Kalia frowned. "Anything more?"

"Half of the page is faded other than for a word or two that make no sense."

"We may never know. Why weren't copies of these books and records made?" Her sigh showed her exasperation. She opened another book. "This is the one where I read about the strange bracelets." Slowly she turned the page. "Here."

"You read and I'll write." He dipped a quill into the inkpot.

"Four Guilds. Four metals. Gold for the Healers.

Lines of Fire

Silver for the Justicars. Electrum for the Artisans. Copper for the Defenders. Wearing bonding bracelets of their metal will enhance their talents. One pair of bracelets with all the metals has been made and will appear when a Guild needs to be reminded of the days of terror beyond the mists.

Bracelets of brass for those who choose no Guild. If any among the commoners show a desire for a particular metal he or she should be trained.

The bracelets of remembrance will appear when there is a need and will guide a particular guild for a time.

Alric put the quill back in the pot. "I wonder where my father found them. Did they guide his desire to see the Defenders return to the ways of the past?"

"We may never know." She closed the book. "When this is done we must return and read all these books."

"Will take more than two of us." Alric returned the volumes to the shelves. He reached for her hand. "Time for the nooning."

Alric held her hand as they walked to the refectory. His presence kept her fears at bay. He chose his usual light meal. Ganor and Sando did the same. So did she. Though she wouldn't be called on to duel, her stomach knotted because of the decision she'd made. Alric wouldn't enter the duel without knowing she was his forever. She sipped kafa and listened to the three men discuss different strategies.

Once all had eaten, the patrols walked to the forecourt. Until the gong sounded they performed exercises to loosen their muscles. The activity kept

Kalia from thinking of the duel.

The deep and sonorous note drew them into a double line for the walk to the salle. As Kalia entered the large arena she saw the observers from the other Guilds were seated already. Students, unassigned Defenders, unbonded men and women walked behind the four patrols. She looked for her mother but failed to see her. Would she arrive?

The four patrols stood on the sand facing the raised platform. The Swordmaster strutted into the salle accompanied by his Seconds. He strode to the raised platform and raised his hands. "I have made an important decision. There are some among us who act against the Defenders by giving assignments where none are needed. Once I perform a long needed act, a purging will begin."

Kalia clasped Alric's hand and sought comfort from his touch. What plans did the accursed leader have?

The Swordmaster leaned forward. "I hereby declare my bond to Saris is broken." He tossed a bracelet on the sand.

Kalia's mother rose from a place before the seats of the leaders of the other Guilds. "If you break this bond you will be banished. I am your third mate. Have the long years since we exchanged bracelets made you forget?"

"Truth," the Justicar said.

"I am heart bonded to you. I will not be cast aside."

"Truth."

The Swordmaster's face turned as dark as his

lines. "Then I issue a challenge to any man willing to face me in a duel. Who will stand against me? Where is my heir?"

Chapter 17

Silence followed the Swordmaster's declaration and challenge. No murmurs rose from those gathered in the salle. Alric's grip on Kalia's hand tightened. Would Robec appear? If he accepted the challenge from his father, would the Swordmaster let him live? The silence dragged on. Tension gathered. Alric steeled himself to wait for events to unfold like the dew kissed flowers of the morning star.

Laughter burst from the Swordmaster. Not the merry laughter of a child but a chilling sardonic sound. "Is there no one willing to duel with me? If not, my will prevails." He snapped his fingers and pointed to the Left Hand. "Bring my former bondmate here." He drew his knife. "I will cut the bracelet from her arm."

Kalia's body shook. She gazed into Alric's eyes. "Stop him."

He brought her fingers to his lips before releasing her hand. "If no one else accepts your challenge, I will. Before we enter the circle to duel, I call for Robec to join me. I will not take his place unless he fails to respond."

From the ranks of the patrols, Robec's name rang out. Once again, the call went unanswered.

"Then the fight is mine," Alric said. "I made a promise to my dying father to see the Defenders return to the ways of the past. For too many generations the power has collected in one line. To break the change I accept the challenge."

Kalia stepped to his side. "Before the duel begins, before those gathered here, I say these words. I am heart bound to Alric and will be his forever."

He held their hands aloft. "As I am heart bound to Kalia. I promise forever."

The Swordmaster glared. "This foolish gesture won't change what will happen. We will fight to the death. When I win, the bond to my mate will be broken. Also Kalia, so will yours. You will serve Petan who will stand at my side and be named as my son." He beckoned to Alric. "I offer you a chance like your father had. Break your bond with my daughter. Take your bihorn and ride as far and as fast as you can before you perish by my blades."

Alric stared at the older man. His lines of fire barely moved. They appeared as ribbons of black marble. "Among the Defenders are those who can see the lines of fire flowing over a man's or woman's skin. The Swordmaster's are dark and tainted."

"Truth," the Justicar shouted.

Scattered yeas spread among the audience. "We see," rose from the patrols.

The Swordmaster laughed. "Not tainted."

"False."

"The lines I now bear give me unlimited power. You do not know how matters with the Defenders progress. Speak no more. My years of experience and the number of duels I've fought have darkened my lines." He gestured to his Seconds. "Will you who have followed my orders for many years stand with me? We can defeat this challenge and keep the Defenders strong."

Alric waited for the answers. Tension crept along his spine like the movement of inchworms across the ground. How many years had passed since the leader faced a true challenge? The Swordmaster's father, grandfather and several greats had ended their role as leader in a sham duel. If Robec appeared, would the Swordmaster permit his son to win?

The Left Hand bowed. "I will not stand with you. A change is sorely needed. You have neglected to order the patrols into the east sector to capture the outlaws terrorizing the people we swore to protect."

The Right Hand rose. "I will not stand with you. Since the day your closest friend was banished we have walked together. On that day I remained silent for I wanted his place. I can no longer remain at your side. You did nothing to protect my daughter from the wiles of your favorite. Your son has always been second in your esteem. The child I foolishly rescued has taken Robec's place. Alron was right. Petan should have been fostered."

The Swordmaster's face turned as dark as his lines. "When I win I'll challenge both of you." He stood taller. "Now I banish you both. Leave the Hall."

In the stands, nine men rose. The leaders and seconds of the other Guilds faced the podium. The Justicar raised a hand. "You issued a challenge and were answered. Until the duel ends you have no right to banish anyone. You know the rules set by the Defenders when they crossed the mists. Those rules were designed to fight the sorcerers lest they rise again."

Alric straightened. Had a sorcerer followed

them or had one risen from among the commoners?

"Then I will fight but not alone," the Swordmaster shouted. "Robec, come forward and join your new found power to mine."

A stir moved through the audience. Alric turned a full circle searching for the leader's son. He spotted a man entering the salle. His hands tightened on the hilt of his sword.

"Robec won't come," Petan said. "He is a coward and fears what was given to him by one, more powerful than we are. Swordmaster, I'll stand at your side only if you promise when Alric dies, Kalia will be mine and I will be your successor."

"Since Kalia was promised to you before her ill-chosen match, the promise of her as your mate stands." The Swordmaster's lip curled into a cruel smile. "As for the other, when the duel ends I'll declare you my heir once there is a grandson of my line." He moved to the Seconds. "Make the circle double."

When Ganor stepped forward, Alric shook his head. "You don't have to stand with me. I've fought two before."

"But I will. My decision comes from within. Neither man will follow the formal patterns."

Kalia pressed her lips to Alric's. "You must and will win."

"I hope so." He removed his vest and shirt. While she folded them, he removed the chain holding the bracelet. "When the duel ends we'll exchange the common bracelets for this one until copper ones are made." He bent to kiss her.

"Fight wisely," the patrol members shouted.

Alric took his place in the circle and studied his opponents. The lines of fire on the Swordmaster's skin barely moved. Petan's flowed but not with the vitality as Alric's and Ganor's. The circle was formed to the largest size. Alric and Ganor stepped over the sand filled leather sacks marking the boundary.

"Ready?" Alric asked.

"As ever." Ganor replied. "I'll fend off the Swordmaster. You see to Petan."

The Justicar and the Artisan examined the swords and knives of the men. Then the pair mounted the raised platform to act as judges. The Chief Healer and his Seconds stood at the edge of the circle.

"Begin."

Alric nodded to Ganor. They separated and slowly advanced. The Swordmaster and Petan stood less than a sword length apart. Both men charged forward. Alric moved toward Petan. He knew Ganor would take the Swordmaster, especially with the sluggish movement of the leader's lines.

Petan's lines of fire telegraphed his coming actions. Alric drove the other man back. Ganor and the Swordmaster exchanged a flurry of blows. The older man retreated and stepped too close to his partner. On a back swing Petan struck the Swordmaster's abdomen. The older man stumbled and fell. Blood pooled around him. Petan leaped aside.

"Time," the Justicar called.

Alric wondered if Petan's action had been an accident or deliberate. He kept his gaze on his opponent and moved aside to drive the action away from the fallen man. Ganor dragged the Swordmaster to the edge of the circle where the Healers waited.

Petan charged. Alric focused his attention on avoiding a singing blade and a jabbing knife. During a feint Alric knocked Petan's knife from the circle. Alric sliced his knife across his opponent's thigh near where he hoped was the place Kalia had stuck her knife days before. A lucky blow cut across Alric's knife arm. He danced away and took a moment to halt the bleeding.

The slash on Petan's thigh made his gain awkward but he continued to attack. His lines of fire grew sluggish. Alric saw his chance to end the duel. He battered Petan with a series of blows driving the man back until Petan fell over the sandbag barrier onto the sand beyond the circle.

"Duel ended," the Justicar and Artisan shouted. "Alric is the winner."

"Send Petan to the Isle," a man shouted.

Alric lunged after Petan and nearly landed on the barrier. Petan ran toward the exit. "This isn't over. I will return and face you again. My master wants the Defenders to be mine."

Alric watched Petan vanish. Though Alric wanted to end the threat the other man posed, by the time he made his way through the people milling around the Swordmaster his enemy had vanished.

The Justicar raised his hands. "A new Swordmaster now guides the Defenders. What sentence will you pronounce on the defeated?"

"None not already in place," Alric said. "Petan was vanished weeks ago. The Swordmaster's fate isn't mine to judge." He left the circle and walked to where Kalia argued with her mother.

"You will not touch him," the older woman said.

"Mother, I can stop the bleeding. If the flow isn't halted he will die soon."

"He has chosen his own fate. He's mine and I will decide how and when he crosses the abyss."

"Meral." The Swordmaster's voice rasped. "I bind my heart to you as I should have done years ago when I desired what my friend possessed."

She knelt at his side. "I can heal the blight now but it's too deeply embedded to spare your life." She pressed her lips to his.

Alric gasped as the Swordmaster's lines slowly cleared. Each one flared scarlet for a moment before vanishing. So did the matching lines of his heart bound mate.

Kalia stepped forward. Alric caught her shoulders. "You can't help."

She turned and pressed her face against his chest. "Why not?"

"The choice isn't ours. We haven't been asked for our help." He drew her closer. "I failed to help my father for the same reason. He never asked me to spend his lines to heal him."

The last bit of darkness left the Swordmaster's lines. Kalia's mother laid her head on her bondmate's chest. Kalia's tears soaked Alric's chest. He raised her chin. "He is at peace and so is she. The bodies must be prepared for internment."

Robec raced toward them. Had he been in the stands the entire time refusing to answer his father's call? Alric looked at the other man's lines of fire and saw they hadn't changed since the last time he'd seen them. He released Kalia to her brother's arms and turned to the Seconds.

"Will you banish us for our failure to support the Swordmaster?" the Left Hand asked.

"You did what you thought was right," Alric said. "I thank you for standing aside."

"Will you remove us from our roles?" the Right Hand asked.

Alric shook his head. "Until I learn more about how the Defenders were in the first days after our arrival, I'll need your help and experience. Until I find others to stand at my side I hope you will remain."

"What about Ganor and Sando?" the Left Hand asked.

"Neither wants to leave the patrol." Alric smiled wryly. "Neither do I."

The Right Hand nodded. "I will serve. My father told me a tale. Once there was a council made up of the Swordmaster, the Seconds and all the patrol leaders who were in the Hall."

"Then after a day of grieving I'll call a council to meet. Thank you." He turned to Kalia and Robec.

* * *

Kalia clung to her brother. Grief spilled between them. Their father's rule had ended. He had died with clean lines and she could think of him with love again. But her mother had joined his dive into the abyss. Had the ending been worth the price?

A new thought cut through the sadness. Her

mother had heard the words she'd always wanted. Amid the grief, Kalia felt a moment of joy. Did her mother's sacrifice mean the Defenders could change?

Petan remained alive. He would return. She knew that and rubbed her arms.

"You all right?" Robec asked.

"Just thinking of Petan's threat and what that could mean."

Robec stiffened. "He was never my friend. I know that now. Do you believe he will come back here, especially when everyone knows what he has done?"

"Yes, and he'll bring this master he speaks about."

Robec stepped away. "He told me I'd been chosen by one greater than all men. That's why my lines are darkening."

"So were mine." She looked up and saw Alric. She held her hand for him to clasp.

Alric slid an arm around her waist. "The bodies are being prepared. When they are, we will go to the crypt to honor them."

"Honor?" Robec said. "For our mother yes, but our father lost his honor years ago when he surrendered to the blight."

"You're wrong," Alric said. "His lines were clear when he died. He told your mother the words she wanted to hear."

Kalia nodded. "She sacrificed herself to save him. Their hearts were bound in death."

"But he didn't tell us what we need to know," Robec said. "Why did he accept the taint? Why did he allow Petan to steer his life and decisions?"

"There was no time to ask." Kalia clasped her brother's arm. "Petan knows the answers. We must find him."

"That will be my quest." Robec squared his shoulders.

"You will have another search," Kalia said. "One to take the taint away."

"How? Every time I worry or think about Petan, the darkness grows."

Kalia nodded. "I know what the dark emotions can do to the lines. Mine are clear again. Remember what we told you. Alric and I have a double heart bond. Seek the one for you."

"Here?" Robec made a face. "I've met every unbonded woman residing in the Hall. None interest me." He turned to Alric. "Since you're the Swordmaster give me leave to wander on detached duty."

Alric nodded. "You have my hope for success. Before you leave, spend time in the Archives. Learn what you can about this infection, heart bonding and the sorcerers our people crossed the mists to leave behind."

Robec's mouth gaped. "Do you think one of that ilk came here?"

"Yes."

Kalia clasped Alric's and Robec's hands. She nodded in agreement. "Tomorrow I'll help with the search." She turned to Alric. "Do you recall which book you found that reference?"

"The second one you gave me."

The Right and Left Hands approached. "The women have cared for the body. The crypt has been opened."

Alric turned. "Kalia, you and Robec will lead the way." He struck the summoning gong five times. From the patrols, the leaders and their seconds approached. The litters with the bodies were lifted and the procession began. The people of the Defender's Hall marched in orderly lines from the salle, across the forecourt, through the gates to the crypt where the bodies of the dead were placed.

Alric, Robec and Kalia followed the men bearing the bodies into the building. They helped move the corpses onto a shelf bearing the bones of those who had died in the past. Some of the bones had turned to dust.

Kalia wrinkled her nose. The stale odor of the crypt made her feel ill. She clasped Alric's hand and followed him into the sunlight. Robec stumbled after them.

Alric raised his hands to address those gathered around the opening. "The Swordmaster and his heart bound are at peace. Before you return to the Hall and continue your day, Kalia and I want you to witness our exchange of bracelets marking our pledge of forever."

Kalia stood beside him. "We will tell you the meaning these special bracelets have for Defenders. We discovered the information in the Archives."

Alric clasped the bracelet with links of four metals on Kalia's arm. She did the same for him. "They are bracelets of remembrance. This is what I read. Copper is for the Defenders. Other metals belong to the other Guilds. From this day forward, all bonding bracelets for our guild will be made of copper."

"What if we want to wear the ones we have

worn since the day of our bonding?" A woman's voice rose from the mass of people.

Kalia smiled. "Wear them. Copper ones will be exchanged and will distinguish the Defenders from the other Guilds and from the common people." She turned to Robec. "You can't leave until you have a pair. Lasara found two hidden in a storage place in the floor of the chamber that was mine."

He nodded. "I'll stay until then."

Kalia smiled. "Tomorrow, Alric will speak to the Artisans and I will show you the ancient records."

Alric raised his hands. "Tomorrow I'll meet with the Seconds, the patrol leaders and their seconds. We'll plan our strategies for handling a band of outlaws. There are records to be copied. Think of the members of your patrols who will be best suited to the task." He pulled Kalia toward the gate. "We should examine the Swordmaster's suite."

"Can we wait several days and use your suite until the room can be cleaned and the furniture moved?"

"We can." He turned and waved the patrols and people toward the gates.

Kalia strode beside him. They stopped in the refectory where he loaded a tray with a selection of food. She took a pitcher of kafa and one of citren. They hurried to his suite. Alric put the tray on the table and took the pitchers from her.

"What's the rush?" she asked.

"To avoid questions I'm not ready to answer and to be alone with you."

She laughed and stepped into his embrace. Their

mouths met. Tongues tangled. She savored his taste and inhaled his musky scent. When the kiss ended, she touched his lips with her fingers.

Alric released her. He stripped off his clothes before she had a chance to remove more than her vest and shirt. When he scooped her into his arms, she laughed. "So eager."

"Always for you. Time to make up for the interruption this morning and to celebrate a most eventful day."

She brushed her hand along the place where Petan's knife had cut his arm. "Does this hurt?"

"No and the Artisans checked the knife so there was no hidden filth to cause a problem."

Kalia smiled. Their lines of fire moved in unison. The currents of scarlet seemed to cross the barrier of their skin, blending and returning like the thrust of their tongues. She rolled to her back and he moved above her.

"You have my heart," she said.

"And you have mine."

His lips brushed her throat and returned to her mouth. With one movement he entered her channel. She tightened her inner muscles. Mutual movement carried heat, called passion and ended in an explosive storm of love.

With a loud roar of her name, he gathered her close and rolled to his side. The savage kiss changed to a gentle tasting.

"Forever." The word etched in scarlet danced before her eyes for they had spoken in unison.

* * *

One week, then two passed before the copper bracelets arrived from the Artisans. The reddish brown metal gleamed in the light from the glass panels in the ceiling of the salle. Kalia and Alric joined the couples on the sand and dropped the bracelets, both the brass and the multi-metal ones on the heap. After clasping the copper ones on each other's arms, they spoke the vows of forever with the others.

Kalia smiled. Not only had she and Alric exchanged their bracelets but the seconds plus the patrol leaders and their seconds. A number of other members of the Defenders also made the exchange. Their gasps of surprise echoed hers. The lines of fire on their skin seemed visible to the world.

Alric raised his hands. "Dismissed."

Robec paused and selected a copper pair. "I'll be leaving in the morning."

"Join us in the refectory," Kalia said.

Before following the men, she looked for the bracelets with the four different metal links in the pile of brass. They had disappeared. For a moment she wondered which Guild would be next. That wasn't her problem. The Defenders had enough to solve.

Once through the line with their trays, Kalia chose a small table. Robec carried his tray. She patted his hand. "I'll miss you." She noticed his lines remained unchanged. "I wish you good fortune."

He met her gaze. "I learned so much in the Archives but all this knowledge is jumbled."

"You'll find the right end and unravel the facts,"

Alric said. "Remember calmness is the way to keep the darkness from growing."

"Where will you go?" Kalia asked. "If you see Lasara, tell her she can return. She needs to know about Mother and Father."

"I'm not sure that's the way I'll travel," he said.

"Will you go east since that's where Petan has collected his band of outlaws?" Alric asked.

"Perhaps." Robec bent his head and concentrated on his food.

When they finished the meal, Robec rose. "I'm off to gather my supplies."

Alric handed him a purse heavy with coins. "To keep you from needing a pack train."

Robec laughed. "My thanks."

"Be careful," Kalia said.

"I will."

"There will always be a place for you here." Alric clapped Robec's shoulder.

Robec kissed Kalia's cheek. "I will return and my lines will be clean." He turned and strode away.

Alric reached for Kalia's hand. "He'll succeed and he will find his heart bound mate the way I found mine."

She leaned forward and touched her lips to his. She felt their lines of fire unite. "Forever."

The End

About the Author

Janet Lane Walters is a multi-published award winning author. To date she has published 35 novels, 10 novellas, 4 non-fiction books, and a number of short stories and poems. She lives in the scenic Hudson River valley, a setting in many of her novels. She bills herself as the eclectic writer and writes romances, from sweet to spicy, cozy mysteries, alternate world fantasies, historicals, paranormals and fantasy from YA to adult. She is the mother of 4 and the grandmother of 7. She lives with her psychiatrist husband who has no desire to cure her obsession with writing. Among her hobbies are Astrology and composing music. She also admits to housework as a hobby for isn't that what one does in their spare time.

Books We Love books by Janet Lane Walters
Gemstones
Code Blue
Choices
HeartThrob
The Doctor's Dilemma
A Double Opposition

YA books by J.L. Walters
Affinities Escape
Affinities Havens
Affinities Searches
Affinities Confrontations

Note from the Publisher:

Thank you for purchasing and reading this Books We Love eBook. We hope you have enjoyed your reading experience. Books We Love and the author would very much appreciate you returning to the online retailer where you purchased this book and leaving a review for the author. Best Regards and Happy Reading, Jamie and Jude.

Books We Love Ltd.
http://bookswelove.net

* * *

Top quality books loved by readers,
Romance, Mystery, Fantasy, Young Adult,
Vampires, Werewolves, Cops, Lovers.

* * *

Looking for Something Spicier
for Sexy Spicy Selections
Books We Love Spice
http://spicewelove.com

Made in the USA
Charleston, SC
21 July 2013